S0-ARB-665

WHEN SH*T GOES SOUTH

HER PRIORITY, HIS OPTION

L. DARSELL

When Sh*t Goes South: *Her Priority, His Option*

This book is a work of fiction. Names, characters, situational descriptions are used fictitiously.

ISBN: 978-0-99977-910-1

THIS BOOK HAS BEEN A JOURNEY YEARS LONG. I'M THANKFUL TO MY CIRCLE OF FAMILY AND FRIENDS WHO'VE DONE EVERYTHING FROM REVIEW, EDIT, ENCOURAGE AND POUR INTO ME TO FINISH WHAT I STARTED. TO ALL OF MY M'S – MY LOVE FOR YOU IS FOREVER. MY FAMILY, BY BLOOD OR NOT, THANKS FOR ALL YOU DO.

1

Six foot-three inches, 230 pounds well-toned in all the right places ~ muscular arms, nice pecs bubbling underneath his fitted shirt, calves to die for that were exposed at the hem of his cargo shorts, and the big feet that weren't part of the myth! This walking cup of Godiva hot chocolate with his smooth skin and sensual eyes that were having an affair with the sun in the open-air space, shifting colors with the lights' reflection, was turning the heads of all the ladies and an occasional man. You could see he invested as much time in his clothing as he did his body – a walking orgasm for sure.

Damn!!! Who is that? Elyce thought to herself. *He looks good enough to fuck right here in the middle of this food court. Gotta be a playboy type for sure. If he keeps looking at me, I'm going to set it off in here.*

Xavier Tuft knew he had it going on in the looks and physique department, but he also had the intelligence, charm and a smooth tongue to match. On a cool fall day in September, while strolling through the mall, he saw her. This fine sister with full lips, full hips, and a smile that stopped him dead in his tracks. He'd watched her as she perused the stores in a hot pink sundress that moved from left to right as her cheeks did the same. Her tapered haircut shaped her round face perfectly while her teardrop earrings and square framed glasses perched up on her head added to the beauty she exuded. While he wasn't the only one starring at the lovely vision, he knew he had to attempt to get her attention. He continued to walk in her direction, staring at her, hoping she would notice.

"It's not polite to stare and not speak!" the sweet

voice said as she approached Xavier. "Hi, Mister…what's your name?"

"Uh…oh, my bad, beautiful. It's Xavier, Xavier Tuft."

"Is that Tuff or Tuft?"

Xavier smiled, showing his perfectly aligned teeth. "That's T-u-f-t, beautiful."

"Well hey, Mr. Tuft," she said as she extended her hand to him. It was the most attractive hand he had ever seen and very soft.

"Thanks for the compliment but you may call me Elyce."

Captivated by her presence he gave her a nice handshake and, to his surprise, this beautiful being had a unexpectedly firm one, one that made him embarrassed that he had given her such a wimpy grip. And just like that, she let go of his grasp, and proceeded towards the mall doors. Xavier was left stunned and disappointed while being equally pleased with the rear view of Elyce. As she sashayed away, she looked over her shoulder and in a voice that sounded like a warm island breeze she sensually said, "Have a wonderful day, Xavier."

The way she said his name sent chills through his spine.

"Damn!" Elyce overheard Xavier exclaim. "I didn't even get a number or a last name." Though Elyce never stopped her stride, a mischievous smirk came over her face. She smiled as she put on her shades while thinking to herself, *it was very nice to meet you, Mr. Tuft.*

"Dog, I'm tellin' you, she was fine! I lost my cool and all my charm obviously went elsewhere because she just walked off…without me."

"Mr. Mack Daddy, you? Mr. Adonis, you? Wassup with you? It's out of character for you to miss a chance to put the Xavier mystique on her. What happened?" Xavier's buddy, Niko, asked laughing. Xavier closed his eyes and visualized the heavenly queen.

"Elyce." Even the way he said her name was like a little schoolboy with a crush on the cute girl in class. Except this time, he visualized her where she should be, with him, instead of walking out the mall doors like she just did a few hours ago. Niko slapped the table causing Xavier to regain focus.

"Really? You trippin' over a chick and all you know is her first name? You need to refocus. Let's go hoop. Maybe that will get Ms. Beauty out of your head. Get changed."

"You're right. I'm trippin. I don't even know this chick and the odds are I will never see her again. Give me a minute to get changed," Xavier said with a long exhale looking as if he'd missed his one and only chance.

Just as Xavier was thinking about Elyce, she was recounting the chance encounter as well to her girl.

"What the hell do you mean you just walked off from a fine ass man like that? Are you crazy? He was sweating you and you walked away?" Jayce asked.

"Girl, please! All that glitters is not gold. We have both dated enough aluminum foil to know that. He was too damn cute and he's probably running women in and out of his house every night, mad they can't watch the sunrise! I ain't trying to be part of no dudes' pussy harem. If I can't have priority seating in the front, I ain't ridin'. Been there; done that. Being a willing option is played out. I'm so over it. He might work for an occasional 'ride' – no strings attached – you know what I'm saying?" she yelled out to her friend who was still down the hallway in her bedroom getting ready for their outing. "Now, get your purse; we're going to be late for the movie."

"Well, you do have a first and last name, Elyce. Google his fine ass and if you don't, I will. It's funny that his first name is your last name too!"

"Good point, about searching for him and yes, that whole Xavier thing is crazy." Elyce laughed at her friend's suggestion, "but all that will have to wait. I can't get all caught up before the mofo is even caught. Now let's go, the movie starts in 20 – with your slow ass."

"Whateva, heifa," Jacye said as she grabbed her shades and walked on past Elyce. "The way you drive, we'll make it in plenty of time."

A week had passed since that trip to the mall. Elyce sat in her bed watching *Love Jones* for the umpteenth time quoting all her favorite lines, especially the one about falling and a dick.

"Shit, I'd like to fall on Mr. Fine's dick right now," she mumbled to herself. She had images of Xavier holding her, caressing her skin and making her…as she snapped out of her daydream she thought there was no time like the present to search for Mr. Tuft on the good old internet.

"Hmmm, I wonder what would happen if I just type 'Mr. Fine' in the search bar?" After pressing enter, she did not like what she saw.

"Oh damn, I get Mr. Not Fine but ugly as hell. Dude stop lying to yourself," she said, cracking a smile to herself. Just as she was about to enter Xavier's name, her phone rang.

"What it is, yo?" Lana said on the other end. "What are you doing, doc?"

"Looking for Mr. Fine on the internet, girl." She pushed the keys correlating to his name, X-A-V-I-E-R T-U-F-T. "Oh wow, there's several listings for him, accomplishments, articles, and social media."

"Well, missy, he's gotta be on one of those listing. Anyway, where is the crew hanging tonight?"

"Girl, I do not know," Elyce sighed. "But whatever it is, it best be good. I'm long over due and Thunder Vibe ain't cuttin' it if you know what I mean."

"Naw fool, I don't know 'cause I gets mine on the regular!" Lana teased.

"You make me sick, selfish ass bitch – you could at least sympathize with me. Let's get the crew on the phone. You call Jayce and I'll call Sienna."

"Hold, please," they both said in unison.

"Hey, Divas!" Elyce called out.

"What do you heifas want?" Sienna said dryly.

"I know, right," Jayce said. "What are you two talking about now?"

Lana smacked her lips loudly into the phone, "Don't you hoes even act like that. Y'all know we haven't kicked it in a minute so its time to get our groove on, flakin' ass bitches."

"Exactly!" Elyce chimed in. "And please believe I need more than a groove. I need some dick, 'mediately, ya heard! I can't stop thinking about that fine specimen I met last week. If I saw him right now, I'd put his hand in my panties, so he'd know what's waiting for his ass."

"Trick, we do not wanna hear that shit," Sienna joked. "Your ass might wanna take care of that waterfall problem and call us back."

"Man, forget you hussies – don't act like you don't know. What time and where because Mr. Bullet is calling me to the shower," Elyce said hurridly.

"Seven-thirty at Sienna's," always punctual Lana said.

"Cool."

Elyce disconnected from her girls and ran to the shower. She pressed the screen on her iPod so she could jam and cum at the same time. As the water splashed on her body, she placed her waterproof toy between her legs and pleasured herself thinking about Mr. Damn Fine.

"Hey, good morning, babe," Xavier said as he caressed the face of his overnight company, Mila. Not one to have a regular chick but enjoyed the company of women on the regular, he had his pick of the litter. "What's for breakfast?"

Almost purring, Mila replied, "you" as she disappeared under the covers.

"Damn baby, again?"

"Um hmm" is all she could reply with his dick lodged perfectly in her wet mouth.

He laid back and enjoyed the sensation that was building in his nuts. As he closed his eyes, there she was, the beauty from the mall. Only this time, she was naked and twisting her body in front of him, making his pelvic thrust up and down as Mila continued to pleasure him. Just as he envisioned Elyce bending over pleasuring herself with her finger inside her, he came hard, toes curled and all.

"Shit! Thanks, ma."

"You're welcome," Mila replied.

Thinking he hadn't said that out loud, he smiled knowing that the compliment was for the vision in his head. He got out of bed and hit the shower.

"What's on your agenda for today?" he asked.

"Wishing I could spend the day in bed with you," she replied.

"No can do, babe; I've got a busy day."

"But it's Saturday, X," Mila sighed heavily as she stood in the doorway of the bathroom watching Xavier clean himself up.

"I know what day it is babe and you know how I do—me, the fella's, and maybe you later. How about for now, you come on in here with me for just a little more X-time?-o0

2

"Hey, what's up? I got caught up with some biz after our game earlier, so I'll meet you and Max at the Rooftop."

Niko hit the end call button on his phone after listening to Xavier's voicemail message.

"Yo Max, let's roll cause that dude will be late for his own funeral man. X is going to meet us at the spot."

"Man, don't that busta know we are hip to his 'I'mma be late' move? He'll be there like five or 10 minutes after us. He just wants to drive just in case he meets a shortie."

"Yeah man, you right," Niko said laughing. "We gon' call is ass out about it too! All he gonna say is, 'fuck ya'll, hatin' muthafuckas! Ya'll trippin! A brotha can't be courteous and not hold you up?'"

"Let's bounce so we can peep the scene first and get the jump on his ass. Won't be no shorties left for him to holla at."

"Talk to me," Xavier said through his speaker phone.

"Hey baby, we on for tonight?"

"Uh, I thought we had this convo this morning already, Mila. I told you I was kickin' it with the fellas and maybe we'd connect later."

"But haven't you been with them all day, Xavier?"

"And wasn't I with you last night and this morning?"

"No, actually after midnight is already morning, babe."

"So, what you saying?"

"I wanna be more than a booty call, X. We haven't kicked it before midnight in weeks. I'd like to catch a movie, dinner, club, something besides a wet ass all the time."

"Whoa babe – is that what you think this is? I'm hurt that you would make it seem like it's just about sex for me. Shit, I don't know why you'd put up with someone who'd make you feel that way. Maybe you should stop seeing me!"

"You get on my nerves, Xavier. Goodbye!"

"Later."

"Hey…call me if we hookin' up later though."

Laughing at her comment, "Ok, Miss Mila. Peace." And with the push of the button she was gone.

Damn, he thought to himself, *she tryin' to lock a brotha down; she's trippin', but the sex is good. Time for a little quality time date to chill her ass out!* X grabbed his keys, checked the mirror and headed out to meet the fellas.

"Alright Lana, I sure hope there's something worth my time or a least a fuck up in this joint tonight!" Elyce said.

"I heard that," Both Jayce and Sienna said at the same time.

"Jinx, bitch!" Sienna laughed. "This spot is supposedly poppin' on Saturday nights. Live DJ and plenty of men with and without dates. At least, that what Lana claims."

"Yeah that's exactly what I said and shit, those chicks up in there don't know me; I will take their man's number and have his ass tomorrow if they ain't careful."

"You are crazy Lana, but we know you telling the truth – seen that shit happen too many times before. Alright divas, let's get the damn money shot and hit it. Somebody is getting got tonight!" Elyce said, pausing in front of the full-length mirror and poking her booty out unnecessarily.

"Bitch, can't nobody miss that big ol' behind – bring your 'need some dick' ass on!"

"Go to hell, Sienna! I hope your ass took a nap, so you can get your swirl on with yo' granny actin ass."

It seemed as if the elevator was bouncing on the way up.

"Ah shit, Elyce, that's our joint right there," Lana said bouncing off the elevator at the Rooftop, waving her hands in the air while the DJ played some old school bangers.

The Rooftop was one of the hottest spots in the ATL. It had the perfect view that overlooked the lights of the park and the surrounding buildings. The colors in the air were so beautiful and it went right along with the people who were there for the music and the laid-back ambience.

"Where's the bar?"

"It's around the corner, Jayce."

"Lana, girl, how did you find this spot?

"I came for dinner at the hotel with a client earlier this week and the bartender told me about it before I left so, I peeped it and knew we had to come back. Ya'll know how we find a spot and make it our own."

"Damn Lana, the skyline is beautiful. We've gotta take a picture; this shit is dope. Glad you got the tip," Sienna said.

"Drink, please!"

"Hold on, Jayce." Sienna saw a group of dudes to her left as they headed towards the bar.

"Say sweetheart," Sienna tapped the stranger's shoulder. "Can you take a picture of me and my girls?"

Niko turned around, caught off guard.

"Damn!"

"Is that a no?" Sienna asked.

"Oh, definitely not! I will take it if you promise to take one with me later." Sienna pursed her lips together, looked him up and down, smiled that killer smile.

"Sure, no problem."

Niko handed his beer to Max.

"Hold this, man, and check out these fine beauties while I take this picture of them." Turning around, he took the camera from Sienna. "Alright lovelies, smile!" The ladies stood sideways for their profile shot with wide smiles.

"Thanks, darling." Sienna gave him a light hug. "I'll catch you in a picture later."

"Bet! And by the way, my name is Niko, and this is my boy, Max. We will see you later for sure."

The ladies turned and headed towards the bar. "Damn Max, did you see them? We can't let any

of them get away. I think I'm in lust!"

"Been a minute again, I see! Don't get stupid and run them off with your whack ass lines," Max said as they both watched the group disappear around the corner.

"Girls, Niko was cute and so was his boy, Max. We need to find a spot that's not too close but not too far either."

"I heard that, Sienna! I guess you trying to get or, shall I say, give up a number."

"You know it, Jayce."

"What can I get for you ladies?" The bartender asked.

"You, after you get off! What's your name sexy?" Lana inquired.

"Tariq, and that can be arranged if you're still here when I get off."

"If not baby, I will be back another time for sure," Lana said. "Blueberry vodka and lemonade please, on you, boo."

"No problem, sexy!"

Lana leaned in and kissed Tariq on the cheek.

"Well damn girl, do you know him like that?" Elyce asked.

Both Lana and Tariq looked at each other and burst out laughing.

"Ladies, this is my fine, sexy ass cousin, Tariq".

"Hey, ladies."

"Hey, Tariq," they said in unison.

"Oh, shit naw! I see that look, you ho-pennies got! Uh uh! He is off limits – take y'all's hot asses on somewhere."

"What? Why you hidin' his fine ass from us?" Jayce asked.

Lana turned to them while Tariq was making their drinks, looking straight at Jayce – "'Cause I know him, and I definitely know your skank asses! Not a fuckin' chance in hell."

"Girl, whatever!" Jayce said. "I'm slippin' him my number. Don't worry, you know I like them a lil' younger. I'll take good care of him – have his ass laying right up here," she said motioning to her breast.

"Here you go ladies," Tariq said, "on me!"

"Thanks, baby boy. Watch these heifas 'cause they'll steal your virginity!"

"Cuz, you've seen me all my life – they ain't got nothing I can't handle," Tariq said, winking at Jayce, who'd laid her hand on her breast as if her heart was pounding.

"We'll see! I'll definitely be back later cutie." Jayce stuck the tip of her tongue in the glass and licked her lips and smiled a mischievous grin. "I wanna see if you taste as good as this liquor does!"

"That's it! Let's damn go!" Lana said nudging them away from the bar and her cousin.

"Bout time you got here, X."

"Yeah man, the DJ is doin' his thang and the honeys – dude, you just missed a fab four that Niko took a picture of."

X scanned the Rooftop nodding in agreement with Max and Niko's assessment of the beautiful women.

"So, where they at?"

"Around the corner at the bar, blanka! Max got your late ass a beer already."

"Cool. Good looking out for a brotha. Y'all see anybody worth my time?"

"Man, are you kidding? Look around you. There's a sea of delight up in here. But you better stay clear of your one-night stand over there." Niko leaned his head in that direction.

"Shit!" X couldn't turn around fast enough. "I think she just saw me." He could feel her eyes on him. "Is she coming?"

"Yeah dude! Me and Niko are gonna step back and let you handle it."

"Ah hell naw, you muthafuckers aren't about to let it go down like that." Just then X glanced up and saw a woman who looked very familiar to him.

"Damn!"

"What's up man?"

"Over there. In the red sundress. That's her!"

"Her who?"

"Niko, that's the fine ass woman I met in the mall!"

"Dog, she was with the honeys I took a picture of earlier. Sorry man, she already gave me her number."

"You lyin! She ain't gave you… "

"I guess your punk ass can't call nobody," X heard a woman say as she sucked her teeth and stood there with her arms folded.

"Oh, um, what's up…um, um"

"Belinda, muthafucka! My name is Belinda."

"I know your name, girl," X said while looking across the roof trying to keep the beauty in his view. "How've you been?"

"Not waiting on you to call back anymore. The dick was good but you ain't all that."

"Oh, I'm not huh? Well, why you got a 'tude?"

"Man, what the hell ever. I just thought we could be friends and kick it sometimes."

"Yeah, we could have kicked it sometimes, Belinda. I just didn't say when sometime would be." She continued to talk but Xavier had begun to tune her out while keeping his eyes focused on the lovely lady across the courtyard.

"Sienna, it looks like picture man and his boy have been joined by another fine ass dude," Jayce said.

"Oh my gosh, that's him! Mr. 6'2", 230, Xavier Tuft, from the mall," Elyce said.

"And your ass walked away? What the fuck, Elyce?" Lana said.

"Girl please, don't you see he already has someone?"

"Uh naw, he ain't with that chick because he hasn't taken his eyes off you. What you think, Jayce?"

"Naw, he ain't with her ass and she don't look very happy. He is definitely not checking for her."

"Hmmm, well let me go make a move on his ass then. Come on, Sienna, walk over there with me."

"Naw, diva, we'll be right along. Go handle that! But don't get your ass beat in the process. That chick looks pretty pissed off."

X saw Elyce heading in his direction and watched her sexy ass approach him. Belinda was still talking. *I wish she'd shut the fuck up and get to stepping!* he thought to himself.

"Excuse me," Elyce said sweetly as she reached up, grabbed Xavier's neck and pulled him close to her, kissing him on the lips.

"Oh no, that heifa didn't do that shit," Jayce said, high fiving Sienna and Lana. "She's real bold tonight."

"Baby, what took you so long to get back?" X asked, going along with the act Elyce started.

"I had to make sure I was still looking good for my boo!"

"Boo?" Belinda rolled her eyes and walked off. "Watch that muthafucka. He ain't shit, ya heard!"

"Hmmm, maybe I should take heed to those words. If you were my man, I would expect you to be straight with me if you were seeing other people. Ain't nobody got time for games. Whelp, my work here is done anyway. You looked like you needed to be rescued. Take care, Xavier."

"Wait!" Xavier exclaimed, grabbing Elyce's arm gently before quickly letting go. "Don't leave; give me a minute to talk to you. This is a second chance encounter and I'm not willing to let you leave me standing here like you did at the mall."

"Is that right?"

"It sure is! So, tell your girls to come on over. Next round is on me!"

Elyce waved her girls over to where they'd seen the fellas earlier while the waitress took their drink orders.

"Xavier, these are my girls, Lana, Sienna and--where the hell is, Jayce?"

"Oh, she went to the ladies room, E. Good to meet you, Xavier," Lana said. "Nice to finally put a face with a name."

"Oh, is that right? So, somebody has been talking about me."

"No, they haven't, Lana is just joking with you." Elyce shot Lana a "bitch shut the hell up!" look.

"Oh yeah, she told me she met this fine mofo in the mall, but she let your fine ass get away. Don't be mad, E – you know I love you, girl," Lana said laughing.

"Go to hell. Anyway, introduce us to your friends, Xavier, before I have to toss my friend off the roof!"

"Well, we don't want that! Sienna, Lana and Elyce, these are my boys, Niko and Max."

"I believe you promised me a picture, Sienna."

"Oh yeah, Niko, I definitely haven't forgotten. When my girl, Jayce, gets over here, we'll ask the waitress to hook us up."

"Just in time for the introductions I take it. Hi fellas, I'm Jayce – nice to meet each of you – especially you, Xavier." Jayce turned to Elyce and winked at her.

Sienna whispered in Jayce's ear, "I ordered you a drink and your ass ain't slick; bathroom, my ass."

"Whatever!" Jayce rolled her eyes at Sienna. "I had some unfinished business at the bar. Tell you all about it later."

"Lana is going to kill you, girl."

"Well I guess we won't tell her then, now will we? When the time is right—if it's right—I will let her know."

The waitress returned with their orders and the group hung out just laughing and talking and getting their dance on until the Rooftop was closing down for the evening.

"Well everyone, it's been real. Thank you for being such good company," Elyce said.

"Yeah, thanks." The ladies chimed in.

"It was so nice to meet y'all and hang out with some cool brothas for a change. Niko, I'll send you that picture 'cause you know we looked cute together."

"You do that, Ms. Sienna. Maybe we can share more than a picture one day."

"Maybe we can. I'm sure we'll be seeing each other again soon. Right, Elyce and Xavier?"

"What?" Both Elyce and Xavier said at the same time. They'd walked ahead of the rest of the group talking and exchanging information with one another.

"She said we would probably see them again soon, Elyce, but you and Mr. Fine were too caught up in each other to acknowledge that," Lana said laughing.

"Hi, Hater! You see me!" Elyce shot Lana the finger on the sly.

"Girl, we ain't mad at you. If you didn't make a move tonight, we were going to have a long talk on the ride home and you know you didn't want that."

"Thanks for a lovely evening, Xavier. Don't pay my drunk ass friends any attention; they are just talking mess as usual."

"That's ok. Your girls are real cool. We'll definitely have to all hang out again. Maybe this time we can get to know Jayce too."

"Once she takes care of that bladder problem," Max chimed in. "Damn girl, every time we turned around you were headed to the bathroom," he added.

"Well, when you gotta go, you gotta go! What can I say? I would have been the fourth man out anyway. Besides, I had to take care of some important business for later on this week."

"Later this week huh," Sienna laughed. "How about later on tonight?"

"Okay!" They slapped five. Sienna already knew Jayce had set up a date with Tariq.

"Lana's gonna beat your ass."

"Shit! She's his cousin, not his mama! By the time we tell her, I will have had him for breakfast, lunch and dinner. I ain't trying to marry him; I just want a young stud to bend my back every now and then!"

As they reached the valet area, the group hugged each other and waited to go their separate ways when the cars arrived.

"Elyce, I'm glad I bumped into you again tonight. Is it okay if I call you this week?"

"I look forward to it. Goodnight, Xavier. Goodnight, Max and Niko. See you again soon."

3

"Oh shit, baby that feels so good!"

Their bodies dripping with sweat the two of them just couldn't get enough of each other as he pressed her back against the wall continuing to delve his tongue in and out of her spot as she clinched her thighs around his neck. Considering it light work, Tariq had no problems keeping Jayce in place with his hands firmly pressed against her ass making sure she couldn't get away as he pleasured her.

"You're going to make me cum too soon! Please stop!"

"I don't think so," he muffled between making her squirm with pleasure. "You were talking all that smack back at the bar and now you want me to stop? I'll be in this pussy all night and I need it nice and wet!"

Tariq carefully moved them from the wall to the bed. "This taste better than any drink and I've got the perfect stir for it."

Jayce closed her eyes tightly as she felt the rush of her orgasm exploding all over Tariq's tongue. He placed soft kisses on her pelvic bone, making his way up her stomach, stopping only to tease her nipples with soft bites. Her heart was beating so fast she could barely catch her breath. Her eyes widened when she felt the length and girth of his manhood enter her slowly.

"Mmmmm hmmmm," she moaned softly with a sensual exhale in Tariq's ear whispering softly, "If you keep this up, I'm going to have to keep you captive between my legs."

He didn't respond, just kept thrusting his throbbing dick in and out of her bringing her to orgasm three more times before he finally let go of all the cum he'd been trying so hard to hold onto while he fucked her for more than an hour. Exhausted, they drifted off to sleep with Tariq still inside of her. The early vibration of Tariq's phone on the night stand startled them both.

"Hello," he grumbled into the phone.

"Hey, baby boy! It's your cousin. What you up to?"

"Damn Lana, do you know what time it is? What do you think I'm doing?" he said slightly agitated at the question. "You know I worked late last night and now you're calling me first thing in the morning!" Jayce turned over to look at him as he closed his eyes, shaking his head at the phone.

"Yes, I know what time it is; but I needed to catch you before you went ghost and I couldn't find you later. Can you come by and help me put some things together?"

"Like what, Lana?"

Jayce turned over and backed herself up until her butt was nestled beside his resting penis. She reached back and started to stroke it slowly trying to rush the blood flow to render him powerless as he tried unsuccessfully to loosen her grip – maybe because he was enjoying her soft hands moving up and down his shaft.

"Never mind – I don't want to know. I'll come as soon as I get up in a few hours."

"Thanks, baby! I love you – you know you're my favorite little cousin!"

"Yes, I know…bye!" Tariq ended the call and dropped the phone on his clothes crumpled up on the side of bed.

"You know you're wrong for what you were doing while I talked to my cousin. You almost made me moan into the phone – aren't you trying to keep this from her?"

"Ssshhhh – I don't want to talk about Lana right now or haven't you noticed."

"Oh, I noticed!" he said as he let his fingers explore her wetness, moving slowly across her clit. Retrieving another condom, he grabbed her thigh and placed it over his side causing her legs to open allowing him to slide right inside her from behind. Pulling her into him tightly, the rhythm of their bodies moved together with Jayce squeezing and releasing him softly trying to make him cum before the sensation of his dick inside of her made her body ache again.

"You're so mean. That shit is feeling too good," he managed to say right before he released.

"Girl, Xavier is fine. You did get his number, didn't you?" Sienna said loudly into the phone.

"Yes, Sienna, we exchanged numbers, but you know I'm not going to call him. I know you saw all of those heifa's eyeballing him last night! And why are you yelling?"

"Oh, Elyce, please. I just want to make sure you hear my excitement. And they may have been wishing they were in your shoes but from where I stood, he wasn't concerned about any of them or us for that matter. He was all in your grill. Buying your drinks, rubbing your back and shit. Humph, I know you thought we didn't see that but me and the crew were all eyes. Don't be an ass; call him."

"Whatever, man. I'll think about it. Moving on. Don't forget our spa appointment this afternoon. You know I need some stress relieved since I ain't getting any," Elyce laughed.

"Well that ain't nobody's fault but your own cause I'm sure ol' dude would have died and gone to heaven if you'd taken him home last night."

Elyce sucked her teeth at Sienna's suggestion.

"I do not have to time to fuck a dude on what wasn't even a first date. Hello!!! Do you hear that non-sense coming out of your mouth of all people? I'm done talking about last night. Goodbye girl; I'll see you at 2:30 – don't be damn late!"

Hanging up the phone, Elyce reached in the drawer for her bullet to pleasure herself. *Soon enough I will get Mr. Tuft in my bed but for now, this will have to do*, she thought, placing the soft buzzing object between her lower lips turning the speed on high before heading into the office.

"Good morning, Dr. Xavier. I hope you had a great weekend," Marie stated. She was the office manager for Elyce's thriving health and beauty practice. "I picked up your favorite juices on my way in."

"Thanks, Marie. I'm going to put this stuff in my office and look at my schedule. Do you know off hand how many surgeries I have this week?"

"I just checked this morning. You have three surgeries scheduled. Two on Wednesday and one on Friday."

"Great! That means final consultations today and tomorrow. Hopefully I can get out of here early then."

"You have plans?"

Marie—who was in her early 60's—sometimes put on her mothering hat and felt she needed to look out for Elyce's well-being and social life, asked.

"Not really, Marie," Elyce smiled. "But thanks for checking on me. And don't get any more ideas about setting me up, please."

"OK, Dr. Xavier. I won't try to set you up. At least, not this week."

The new mail icon popped up on Elyce's screen. She didn't recognize the sender's screen name, bankerman. *Hmmm, this is probably some junk mail,* she thought, *into the trash bin it goes.* Elyce then made a quick call to her girl.

"Hey, Sienna. Are you free for lunch today? I'm open for the most part today."

"Sure, E! Where do you want to go?"

"I don't know. Let's both make some suggestions and figure it by email about 12:45."

"Works for me. I'll catch you in a couple of hours and we can talk about planning our girls' trip. Start thinking about places to go, Elyce – like the islands."

Elyce returned from lunch with Sienna and sat back down at her computer. She told Sienna she hadn't heard from Mr. Fine as of yet and wasn't setting her expectations too high to hear from him because he surely has women. She had another email from bankerman. *Hmmm, this "bankerman" obviously knows me.* Elyce double clicked the email.

Hey beautiful! It seems you didn't receive my other email so I'm sending another one. I hope all is well and that we can get together soon. You have my number and now, my email. Use it! – X.

A smile immediately came across her face and she sat back only to be startled by Marie who was looking at her oddly.

"What's that look about, doc?"

"Nothing, Marie. What's up?"

"Nothing is up. I just came in here to give you some paperwork to sign and here you are grinning to yourself, looking like somebody just said the best thing ever to you."

"You know what, Marie? You let your mind wander too much! I wasn't smiling to myself. Now, give me the papers and leave, please. Thank you, mom number two! Would you mind closing the door please? Thanks, bye, bye," she rambled as she seemed to rush Marie out of her office.

Marie peered at Elyce, spun around and left, closing the door as requested. *Geez, that woman will not be happy until I am,* Elyce thought. *Bless her heart.* Turning to her computer, she felt a little anxious to respond.

*Hi X. I wasn't sure who the email was from. I just figured it was just junk mail…*Elyce immediately hit the delete button. Instead, she picked up her phone debating on whether or not to call him. Xavier had opened the door of communication so what was she waiting on? Maybe it's that instant attraction she had for him from the day she saw him at the mall.

"What the hell; stop being school girlish and call him," she said to herself.

"Hey, beautiful," the deep, sexy voice said on the other end causing a flutter in Elyce's stomach.

"Xavier?"

"Yes, beautiful. It's me."

"How did you know it was me? And I told you before my name isn't beautiful."

"Well, it is to me, Elyce. But fine, if it embarrasses you to have a man call you something other than your name, I understand. And I saved your number in my phone the night you gave it to me."

"Anyway! How are you, Xavier?"

"Better now that you've finally called."

"Are you always this charming?" Elyce asked, laughing. "Is that how you get your women to fall for you off the rip?"

"What? I'm hurt that you'd think this isn't genuine. I'm going to hang up now. Thanks for calling, Elyce."

"What's the matter? Did I hurt your little feelings? And here I thought you were a man; not a little boy."

"Oh, I'm a man alright! When you stop being scared and you're ready to see just how much of a man I am, let me know."

Shit! I know he didn't just say that to me. I am not going down like that. "X, please, don't talk mess you can't back up. You're dealing with a smart woman – not one of these average chicks you might be used to. Don't get it twisted."

"Prove it, beautiful. Meet me for drinks tonight. I know this great little bar that we can kick it tonight, if you're not scared."

"Email me the location and time, mister man, and I will see you later. Bye." Elyce hung up the phone and noticed her palms were a little sweaty. The remainder of the workday couldn't go by fast enough.

Elyce pulled up to the valet, checked her hair and minimal makeup and exited car. She spotted Xavier standing just inside the door with a grin on his face. Approaching the door, he immediately opened it.

"Come on in, beautiful—I mean Elyce. So glad you could join me."

Well, we did agree to meet up. Did you think I would stand you up? Is that why you were standing at the door like a little kid waiting on Santa?"

"Ha, ha! You got jokes I see. Call it what you want, Elyce; I am definitely excited to see you and to get to know you better. Is that a problem?"

Surprised by his straight forwardness, she smiled a little and gave him a hug.

"No, Xavier. It's no problem at all. I like being a gift giver to good kids." She couldn't help but laugh.

"Come on, lady. Let's go sit down before you spend any more time trying to be a stand-up comedian!"

After the waiter took their order, they sipped their drinks and continued to chat. "So, tell me Xavier, what happened in your last relationship?"

"I don't know if that really matters. It was a variety of things."

"Well, let me be clear with you so you know where I stand if things don't matter. I would prefer, if you are going to see other people or whatever that you be straight with me. The consequences of the truth will be much better than if you lie."

"I hear you, Elyce. Loud and clear."

Time seemed to pass by quickly. They both agreed to no phones, just good conversation. Neither of them wanted the date to end, but they both had to work early tomorrow.

"So, Elyce, did I pass the test? Will there be another date? And another and another?" Xavier asked.

"I really enjoyed our time this evening. You picked a great place – the roasted brussel sprouts sealed the deal. I for sure think we can have more dates in the very near future."

"Oh, ok – so maybe the way to your heart is through your stomach then. Good to know."

The pair hugged while waiting for their cars but stopped short of anything but a quick kiss on the cheek.

"Until next time," she added before getting into the car and driving away.

Elyce made a quick stop at the gas station before heading home.

"Hey stranger," she heard a familiar voice say. She turned around to see Justin, her ex.

"Hey you. Fancy meeting you here. What's up?"

"You, of course. How've you been?"

"Great! You?"

"Missing you."

"Liar! Same, Justin. Still full of shit."

"Why you gotta be like that doc? Let's go grab a drink and talk for a minute."

"Talk, huh? Ok."

4

"No, Lana! I haven't told him I do more than just health and beauty. He hasn't really asked and I'm not ready to give him all the details of my life. We've only been going out for two months."

"I think you need to tell him you're a plastic surgeon, Elyce," she responded standing in the bay window checking out the picturesque view of the heated pool and hot tub in Elyce's back yard. "You need to get a feel for where his head really is and find out if he can handle being with a successful, independent woman. You have a lot to offer a man. You can't keep going to dates at his place, girlie!"

"I hear you, girl." She walked over to the window where Lana was standing, handing her one of their favorite drinks—a blueberry vodka with lemonade and basil leaves—before heading out on the deck overlooking the pool. "Our conversations are about other things; our interests, sports, traveling, and things of that nature. You of all people should know when I leave work, I don't want to talk about it. We're getting together tonight. Maybe I'll tell him then."

"Where are you guys headed?"

"Just a quiet evening at his place and mind you, he's not living too shabby for a banker man. He's cooking dinner and we're going to watch movies and cuddle."

"Cuddle my ass. When are you going to see what he's about in bed, girl? You know your ass is drier than a turkey on Thanksgiving!"

"Don't remind me. I've been showing some restraint with him girl. I like him a lot. He's so sweet; a true gentleman and he makes me laugh till my sides hurt. I think he's waiting for me to move first. Maybe tonight I will or won't because I slept with Justin last night."

"You did what and I know you didn't say that piece of shit Justin! I hope you used protection."

Damn, Lana. You went from zero to one hundred real quick. It was nothing; it just happened – nothing more nothing less. No big deal. I'm done with that chapter, again.

"Yeah, we'll see how done you are!"

"Red or white, Miss Lady?" Xavier asked from the kitchen where he was preparing dinner. He knew some of Elyce's favorite foods and he was trying to make sure they were prepared to perfection. He even stopped at one of her favorite spots and picked up a piece of their awesome peach cobbler, more crust than peaches!

"Neither. I see you weren't listening to me when I told you I don't like wine, Xavier. White liquor, yes. White or red wine, no thanks."

"Beautiful, I was listening. I just thought you'd like something a little more mellow instead of something that could leave you on your ass if you had too much. I'd already made you a drink."

"Maybe I want to be on my ass," Elyce mumbled under her breath.

"What did you say, beautiful? I didn't hear that."

"Oh nothing, sweetie. I'm looking forward to dinner. It smells really good in there. How much longer?"

"By the time you wash your hands, the table will be set and ready for you to dine sufficiently."

"Sufficiently, huh? Let me be the judge of that." Elyce winked at Xavier as she brushed past him close enough for him to feel her breast against his arm. He almost bit a hole in his lip trying to get a hold of the urge that was building in his jeans as he watched her beautiful ass walk away in her fitted jeans and heels that caused a slight gap between her legs. Xavier let out a slow and controlled exhale as he made his way over to the table with the food.

"Well beautiful, I know you've only had a few bites so what do you think?"

"It's alright." Elyce smiled. "Just kidding; I'm really enjoying dinner – thank you for making all of my favorites, especially the ribs and fried corn. I guess you do listen but your vision is questionable. This plate was extra full and I ate half of it. If I consume any more, I'll need to do something to exercise this food off of my stomach. You have any suggestions?"

"Suggestions? Me? I don't know. Maybe we can go downstairs and hit the treadmill or something. Are you finished?"

"Yes, I think so. I can always take a to-go plate."

He grabbed her hand and led her to the sofa where soft music was playing, and more candles were burning.

"Since this isn't the treadmill, I can think of something that might be more interesting," she whispered in his ear as she slightly bit his lower lobe. She continued to kiss and nibble until she made her way around to his lips, which she parted with her tongue and kissed him with the passion of a woman in need.

Xavier eased her on top of him as he ran his hands up and down her back. He didn't want to be too presumptuous, but he couldn't resist letting his hand travel down to her ass. He gripped both cheeks firmly but not too hard where it would cause her to stop. When she didn't flinch, he knew it was ok to continue.

"Xavier, do you have a t-shirt or something I can slip in to?"

"Uh yeah, beautiful. Sure. Let me go get it for you. Hold up a second." He got up and headed down the hallway.

She could hear his footsteps on the hardwood floors and the drawers opening on his dresser. Elyce took her shoes off and tiptoed back to where Xavier was, dropping pieces of her clothing down the hallway. Just as Xavier found a shirt for her to wear that wouldn't be too long since his manhood wanted his eyes to see as much of her as possibly, he turned around and there she was. Standing in the doorway wearing nothing but her light blue lace front snapping bra, Xavier could see her brown, erect nipples and her matching thong panties. Her skin was flawless; her stomach pancake flat with a simple hoop piercing hanging from her naval. Damn, his dick was getting hard again. He knew she noticed as he saw her eyes looking at the crotch of his pants.

"I've dropped mine. Why don't you drop yours?" she purred as she walked slowly towards him.

Xavier didn't move at first; it was as if he was frozen in place. She walked up to him, lowered his face to hers and kissed him again unbuckling his pants while he unbuttoned his shirt. As his pants fell to the floor, she immediately felt his penis as he wasn't wearing any underwear.

"Ummm. A free spirit. I like that about you."

“Not as much as I like a woman who knows exactly what she wants.” He picked Elyce up and carried her over to the king-sized bed, laying her on the decorative matching pillows and sheets that were exposed from the comforter being folded halfway back.

“Are you sure about this beautiful?” he asked.

“I’ve been sure about this from the first day I laid eyes on you in the mall. In fact, I can’t believe it’s been two months since that day. Now if you don’t mind, I need some exercise for that sufficient meal you prepared. Let’s do something about that.”

“You don’t have to tell me twice.”

Xavier caressed her face letting his hands travel down to her bra, which he unsnapped with ease exposing her breast. He let his tongue make circles around her nipples until they were at their hardest and she began to moan. He rose up to kiss her while his hand traveled down to her thong that was already wet. He slid it to the side and let his finger explore her wetness as he gently moved it in and out of her.

Wanting to pleasure her even more, Xavier kissed her down her neck, licking her nipples again making his way to her mound with his tongue. He slid her thong off and parted her caramel thighs placing them on his shoulders as she looked down at him lustfully with one hand caressing her own breasts while the other stroked his head softly. Without warning, Xavier licked her clit causing her body to slightly jerk. He knew she was so aroused at this point that there would be no turning back.

“I can’t believe how sweet you taste, beautiful,” he said before he let his tongue continue to explore her sticking it in and out of her.

He sucked on her clit until it was fully engorged, and her breathing was at a rapid pace. He could feel her beginning to arch her back as if she were ready to cum all over his tongue.

"Not yet baby, don't cum; I want it all over my dick while it's deep inside you."

Xavier reached for a condom and opened it. Elyce removed it from his hand, pulled him up on the bed and applied it to his penis with her mouth.

"Damn girl, I like the way you are doing that. What else do you have for me baby?"

"I have me; all of me. Right now, I'd like to feel all of you inside of me."

She climbed on top of him holding his dick in her petite hands stroking it up and down while she eased herself around him letting her hips make figure eights. Xavier held her tightly.

"What the fuck are you doing to me beautiful?" "Sssshhhh, just enjoy the ride, baby," she

whispered as her movement changed easing herself off him until just the tip of his penis rested inside of her before squeezing his dick as she eased her way back down.

Xavier pulled her closer to him, so he could suck her breasts. The intensity of his sucking and his shaft rubbing against her clit with each movement she felt the heat rising within her. She began to breathe harder as she came, begging him to let her have it but he wasn't ready. With a fast move, he turned her over and eased himself deeper inside of her pussy that was so wet from the orgasm she was having. The heat from her juices felt so good, he felt his own eruption creeping up.

"Aaahhhh damn," he breathlessly exclaimed as his dick throbbed intensely as he came for what seemed like five minutes, "this pussy is incredible; I could stay inside it all night long."

"That's exactly what I hoped you would say, baby," she said. "I plan on giving you a night you won't easily forget or easily replace. I think the shower is calling us. Get yourself ready for round two."

5

"Yo, X, we playin' ball today? You know you blew us off last weekend, man; is that what happens when you're getting some GP?"

"GP? Man, what the hell is that."

"If you don't know then maybe you're not getting some 'good pussy'!" Niko laughed. "You're slippin', man! What the hell happened to you?"

"Man, I'm not slippin'. I'm getting GP and still have options. But man, in all seriousness, I'm really feeling Elyce but I'm not sure if she's feeling me."

"Come on, X. Since when do you have questions about whether a woman is feeling you or not?"

"We've been going out and spending a lot of time together. I asked her what she did, and she told me she was in health and beauty."

"Yeah, and?"

"So, I know you're going to think this is crazy, but I looked her up online one night but could only find her professional details. She must have some block or something on her personal pages. I couldn't find anything specific but an address popped up. So, I drove past that address because we've only had dates at my crib."

"And?"

"Man, she's in this mini mansion. It was gated, perfectly trimmed lawn and bushes, four-car garage, a deck that overlooked the pool and jacuzzi."

"So what, man? You sound like some bitch right now; tripping about what a chick does and where she lives. Did you tell her what you did? That you're a vice president at that bank and not some teller? Did you tell her how you were able to afford that nice crib you're living in? What the fuck, man. Get a grip, Xavier."

"Niko, I'm just saying man. What's the story behind her being so secretive?"

"Don't know. What's yours? Why don't you get your balls back and ask her?"

"Alright, alright. I hear you, man. You're right. I should just ask her but there's no way I'm telling her I rode past her house."

"You don't really know if it's her house but that's the most sensible thing you've said. Now, back to the original question, punk: are we ballin' today or what?"

"Maybe later, man; Mila will be over here in a minute and you know that can take a little time."

"You were just talking 'bout feeling Elyce, but you've got Mila coming over? Damn man, do your thing and hit me when you're done laying pipe!"

"Yeah man, later. Mila's at the door anyway."

"Were you busy, X? You sounded like you were on the phone with someone. I hope it wasn't one of your sideline hoes."

"You're here, right?"

"Yes."

"Then, I guess not!"

"Fuck you, Xavier. Why are you always trying to put me down and talk shit? Am I not good enough to be your girlfriend?"

"It's not that, Mila. Don't start trippin'. I'm just messing with you. Of course, you're good enough to be my girlfriend but you know I'm just not that into having one right now. We have a good time together just as we are."

"We have sex, Xavier – that's the extent of our relationship. And even that is becoming few and far between. You must be fucking some other bitches. Are you?"

"Now, Mila, why would you even want to know that? All I need right now is you. Come here, girl."

Xavier pulled her towards him and kissed her neck making his way down to her cleavage which was looking very delicious to him right now. Xavier looked up at her and saw the anger that was once in her eyes vanish; his signal to continue. He led her to the couch and eased her down on top of him unbuttoning her shirt exposing her breast. Taking her nipple into his mouth he sucked it hungrily causing her to moan and the heat between her legs to intensify.

"Oh, X, you know just what to do to get me going. I love that about you. I don't know why we can't be this way forever instead of every once in a while. I know you care about me, right, Xavier?"

"Let me show you just how much."

Xavier kissed her hard and deep letting his hand travel beneath the skirt she was wearing to the moisture in her panties. He eased his fingers inside of her and began to fondle her.

"You like that, baby? You know there's more to come. Just relax, let me take your mind off whatever is bothering you today."

Mila arched her back and bit her lip; Xavier saw a tear fall from her eye. *Shit,* he thought, *she's getting too attached. This could be a problem if she ever sees me out with Elyce.* Sidetracked by his own thoughts he heard his name being called.

"Xavier, Xavier! Where the hell is your mind right now? Why did you stop?"

"It's right here with you baby – mind, body and soul," he lied.

Pulling her up from the couch, he removed her clothes and admired her beautiful body – especially the piercing in her clit that peaked out from her freshly waxed vaginal lips.

"I've been wanting some of this pussy all day. Come on, baby, ride this dick for daddy."

Turning her body around, Mila straddled him easing his dick inside of her, squeezing tightly to assist in pushing down the condom he'd barely had time to put on.

"This pussy sure is wet for me, baby. Did you miss me?"

"Yes daddy, me and her missed you so much. Now, work this thang like you do and give us exactly what we always get."

Mila leaned forward while he grinded in her with one hand caressing her breast and the other teasing her piercing. It was feeling so good to her that she began to buck back on Xavier with an intensity like never before, causing an explosion within her in less than five minutes.

"Damn, girl! I guess you did miss me."

"Shut up, man. Just keep making love to me, X. This is my dick and I want it all right now."

Grabbing her thighs with his dick still deep inside of her, he lifted her up and pumped his way back to the bedroom. Laying her on top of his bed covers, he turned her over and plunged deep inside of her. Mila met his thrusts with her own, wrapping her legs tightly behind his back. Balancing himself on his knees which lifted her ass up slightly, he positioned himself even deeper. He could see her breathing harder and her eyes so tightly closed that he knew she was about to cum again. He felt his own juices begin to make their way into the sheath covering his manhood. As the sweat rolled down his back, Xavier let out a loud grown and came just as she came for the second time. Collapsing on top of her, Xavier laid there, his heart rate accelerated watching her still with her eyes closed. His noticed a message was blinking on his phone so without her noticing, he reached over to read it. It was from Elyce.

Hey X. I'll be in the neighborhood in a little while, I'm going to stop by in about 45 minutes, ok? If you're busy, just hit me back and let me know so I don't waste a trip. You know gas is high again!

"Fuck!" he said, not realizing he'd said it out loud.

"What's wrong, baby?"

"Nothing, Mila. I forgot I need to handle some business before I meet the fellas to shoot hoops. I gotta bounce, baby. Sorry. Maybe we can connect later."

"What the fuck, X. This is the shit I was talking about earlier. You don't have time to spend with me. Don't you love me?"

"Damnit, Mila! I'm really not in the mood for this conversation with you again and again and again. I dig you, girl; but pump your damn brakes – this is not a course for marriage."

"So, what am I to you? Just somebody you call when your balls need to release? Some sideline hoe? What the fuck am I to you, Xavier?"

At this point, Mila was yelling, and tears were running down her face. Not wanting to seem like a complete asshole, he wiped her tears away and just held her.

"Look, babe. I gotta get dressed and I can't be in a fucked-up state of mind so please, let's save this conversation for later."

"Later when?"

"I don't know when, baby. But whenever it is, you'll know what you need to know to make you stop second guessing everything I say. Now, stop crying and let me get you a rag. I promise we'll talk."

"I won't hold my damn breath!" she lashed out angrily. Storming past him stopping only to grab her clothes and head for the door wearing nothing.

"Wait, calm the fuck down. You know you can't go out there with no clothes on." He blocked the door, so she couldn't get out. "Put them on Mila, please."

The tears continued to fall but she put on her clothes half-way and stormed out the door.

"I'll call you later, Mila."

She gave him the finger and kept walking, knowing she'd be awaiting his call.

6

Elyce had to slam on her breaks to keep from hitting the woman who'd darted into the street. She looked at her and saw she was obviously distraught while she was trying to compose herself after what could have been a near-fatal accident. She got out of her car and walked over to her.

"Hey, are you ok? You ran right out in front of me – I could have seriously hurt you."

"I'm so sorry," the young woman managed to say between the gasps of air she seemed to be fighting for. "I just had a fight with my boyfriend and I was distracted. I apologize for startling you."

"Maybe you need to go back inside and calm down. Which house is his – I'll walk you over."

"It's the one on the left – but I'm not going back in there; he pretty much rushed me out. I need to go home as fast as I can," the woman said. "I'm sure I look a hot mess right now and I need a shower. Thanks for your concern. I'll be ok."

"Well, calm down so you can drive yourself safely home. Take care." Elyce walked back to her car which was partially blocking the street and pulled into the spot where the young woman pulled out of.

She sat there for a few minutes because the house she pointed to just happened to be Xavier's. "That fucker! I knew he was seeing other people. I don't know why mutherfuckers continue to tell stupid ass lies for no reason." Just then her phone rang.

"Hey baby. Got your message. What time will you be here? I can't wait to see you, beautiful. Maybe we can go grab something to eat."

Putting her car in drive, Elyce eased out of the parking space. "Oh, you know what baby, I'm going to be a little longer than I thought. Can I get a raincheck?"

"Raincheck? Damn, I was looking forward to seeing you."

"Are you sure about that Xavier; it took you a minute to call me back like you were busy doing something or someone else; were you?"

"Look at you – trying to act like I have time or want to be with anybody but you. I don't want a raincheck; I want to see you."

"Well, maybe later – aren't you ballin' with the boys today? I don't want to have a rushed visit with you. Just call me later, ok. We'll figure something out then. Talk to you soon." She hung up before he could say anything. "Lying ass!"

"Jayce, when I tell you this chick was barely dressed with her tits bouncing around in her too tiny ass bra I am not joking. I don't know what the hell happened between them, but it was obvious that they'd probably just fucked. I need a damn drink. Thanks for meeting me; you know I'm pissed"

"You don't know that, Elyce. Why are you trippin?"

"Don't need this bullshit, girl. I told you when I met him that he was probably some playa ass negro with sideline hoes everywhere. You do recall the chick I had to rescue him from at the damn club. I should have let his ass continue getting grilled by her skank ass. You know, it's crazy because you'd think he'd make better choices but, as I've always said, pussy has no face. From the looks of it, he'll fuck any and everything; if they're giving, he's taking!"

Jayce paused for a moment to collect her thoughts before she made Elyce more upset.

"Well if you feel that way, why in the hell do you think he's seeing you? You ain't no low budget hoe; not to say the other chicks are. But you can't just get mad whenever you feel like it; especially if you all haven't established any type of relationship. Is he your man now?"

"No! But we have a good time together and shit. All I've ever asked him was to be real with me. That does include other women."

"Whoa – are you listening to yourself? Be real with you? What about you being real with him? Has he been to your house? Know that you're a plastic surgeon and not some health and beauty consultant? You're a damn hypocrite, Elyce. Get your shit in check and stop playing games. Maybe you need to start being real too. How much I owe on this tab?"

"I got it. I'm going to leave soon but I need to figure out what my next move is. Jayce, you're a mean heifa but I know you're right. I'm going to stay a little while longer. I'll holla at you later." They hugged as Jayce left the restaurant.

Elyce decided to move from the table and go sit at the bar so she could listen to the music playing and chat with her favorite bartender as he prepared her specialty drink. She needed to think about what her next move was going to be and if she would tell Xavier she'd seen him.

"Looks like someone's having a hard day," the sexy voice said as he eased in the chair next to Elyce.

“Like you wouldn’t believe.”

“Well I’d offer to buy you a drink, but it looks like you’ve got two already.”

“Thanks for the offer.” Elyce finally lifted her head out of her hands to look at the gentleman talking to her.

Shit, what a nice distraction. Even though he was sitting, she could tell his body was banging the way his cotton button down fit across his chest nicely and his jeans were fitting in all the right places.

“Like what you see?”

Hearing but not hearing him; she focused on his sexy ass lips and saw them moving.

“Oh, I’m sorry, what did you say?”

“I asked if you liked what you see? I’m Lance, by the way.”

Smiling but not answering at first because her brain and her mouth weren’t on the same schedule.

“Well Lance, I’m the kill-joy of the afternoon. Just call me bad company.”

“I hope you’re not that bad; I’d like to sit and get to know you for a minute. This is my first time in this spot and, since you seem to have a rapport with the bartender, I’m guessing you know this place pretty well. What’s good here?”

“The food is American with a Caribbean flare – the blackened tilapia over rice is really good; so is the guava jerk chicken; oh and the peach cobbler – the bomb! But I’m sure you have a menu; you should really check it out.” She turned to take another sip of her drink.

“And what is that you’re sipping on? From the looks of the sugar rim, it must be sweet. Are you?”

"Am I what?"

"Sweet?"

"Depends on who you ask, the situation, the person, etc. You know what I mean?"

"Yes, I think I do. Well, what do you say, 'bad company'? Will you stay and break bread with me? Maybe I can help you with whatever is bothering you."

"You're kidding, right?"

"Not at all. Come on…what's your name, please?"

"Elyce."

"Come on, Elyce, just sit here with me and let's have a friendly meal – my treat. We'll have your choices and we can share the cobbler."

"OK, ok, ok, Lance. You've been warned but it seems you're determined to have me eat with you. I've already eaten, but I'll join you for dessert."

It wasn't long before Elyce was laughing and joking with her new male friend, but she found herself still thinking about Xavier.

"I've been here way too long, Lance. I should be going. Maybe we can get together and do this again sometime; you were just what I needed. A friendly face, good company, and you're paying the bill. Next time, I will treat you."

"Sounds like a date; well, maybe not a date in the true sense of the word – or is it?" he asked.

"We don't have to define anything right now. I had a good time, you had a good time so let's call it friends. Let's exchange information and stay in touch. Later, gator!"

“Yeah, Elyce, later.”

He watched her as she walked out the front door near the bar – damn, she was fine as hell. He wished he could have gone home with her.

“Say, Rick, what do you know about the lady that just left here? Y’all seem to have a good relationship.”

“Sorry, man. I don’t know her outside of her coming in here with her girls and requesting that I make her drinks. She’s really sweet and personable so, if you’re looking for a hit and quit, I’m not sure you’ll get that from her.”

“Well, one never knows. I’ll just have to wait and see what’s up. Thanks for the drinks and food, man, and tell the brothers that own this place it’s a real cool spot. I will be back. What’s my damage?”

As she approached her car, Elyce reached for her phone to make a call.

“Hey mom, what’s up?”

“Hey, my pumpkin, what’s up with you?”

“Nothing much. Just leaving a restaurant; had a drink with Jayce earlier but she had to leave so I stayed a while longer and met a nice gentleman and had dessert.”

“Husband material?”

“Mom!”

“Hey, I’m just asking. You know your dad and I have been waiting to get that call one day saying you’re getting married.”

“Well, that doesn’t seem like it’s going to happen anytime soon. But I promise you’ll be the first to know as soon as I find a guy who can be with just me.”

"What does that mean, Elyce? Are you seeing someone?"

"No, not really mom. At least, not anymore. Hey, are you guys gonna be in town next weekend – being retired jet setters and all?"

"No, we'll be down at the house in St. Croix, but you are welcome to come down and hang with us. You know we have the room. Bring a friend."

"OK, mom, that's a deal. I love you – tell dad I love him. Gotta go, my phone is beeping. Hugs and kisses."

"Bye, baby."

7

Elyce phone rang, again.

"Ugh, Xavier," she sighed heavily before answering. "Yeah, what's up?"

"Hey girl, where you hiding? I thought we were getting together later. What happened to ya? I been missing you all day."

"Oh really? You've been missing me?" Giving him that hint of sarcasm. "I find that very hard to believe, being that you were otherwise occupied earlier today."

"Huh? Baby, what are you talking about? I wasn't occupied earlier today other than ballin' with the fella's. Plus, you were coming over so how could I have been?"

"Funny thing happened to me today. I was driving down the street and almost hit this woman who darted out in the street. Her clothes were all disheveled and she was crying. I got out the car because it scared me, and she said she'd just had a fight with her boyfriend. Wanna guess what street I was on and what lying mutherfucker she was referring to?"

"Babe…hold on a minute."

"No, I'd rather not. Fuck you, Xavier. I understand we are not a couple and that you obviously see other people – albeit denying that you are—and I probably shouldn't be mad but I'm mad as hell. So, I'm going to be polite right now and tell you I'm hanging up, liar."

"You're one to talk about lying?"

"What did you say?"

"You heard me. We need to talk, doctor."

"Ha! Oh, so you know I'm a doctor – big fucking deal. And for the record I didn't lie; just hadn't got around to full disclosure. Wanted you to get to know me for me – not for what I do for a living. And by the way, asshole, me not telling you what I do doesn't compare to you fucking another bitch; making her run out of your house half-clothed. Look, I don't wanna deal with your shit tonight. When I'm ready, if ever, I'll call you but don't hold your damn breath."

"Wait, hold up. Elyce. Shit!" She'd hung up on him before he could say another word.

Elyce sat in her car with tears rolling down her face but for what? She wasn't his girlfriend so what the hell. A tap on the window startled her. Trying to wipe her tears away she rolled down the window.

"Damn, girl. Was I that bad that you're out here crying over me?" Lance flashed that big grin showing those beautiful teeth.

"Lance, hey. No, nothing like that at all. It's just so typical of my life right now. But I'm good. Thanks for checking on me."

"I can see you home if you like. And that's as a new friend, Elyce, nothing more."

"That's sweet of you but I think I can manage. But I tell you what, I will call you as soon as I get there so you'll know I made it safely."

"Bet. Please do that. Don't have me sitting up worried about you."

Elyce managed to smile at Lance.

"Good night. Thanks for being a real sweetheart. I promise to call or text. Now, watch your toes before I run them over."

"Well, I'm looking for a good nurse and if you crush my feet, part of my lawsuit will be that you come and take care of me twenty-four hours a day; seven days a week; 365 days a year."

"Hmmmm, that doesn't sound like a bad gig! Bye, Lance and thanks again for the company." Giving him a wink as she eased out of the parking space.

"Yo bruh. I got here as fast as I could. What the hell is up? I thought you were meeting up with your girl Elyce tonight."

"Man, Niko, I fucked up bad. Me and these bullshit hoes may have cost me a good woman!" he exclaimed with his head lowered.

"What happened, X?"

"Mila happened! She showed up, we got busy then ol' girl E sent me a text saying she was gonna be in the area and would stop by if I wasn't busy and to hit her up if it was a problem. So, I immediately wanted Mila to leave and kinda rushed her out – which resulted in a fight and her storming out. Well, I went back to my bedroom to see how soon Elyce would arrive, but she was already here and saw Mila leaving the house. They briefly had words because Mila ran out in front of her car, saying she'd just had a fight with her boyfriend – somehow identifying me!"

"Damn, dog!"

"Oh, but get this. Elyce played it real cool acting as if something came up and we'd connect later. Then when I call her, she goes off – like 'muthafucker this' and 'don't hold your breath; I'll call you when I get ready.' Man, I didn't see her as one of my sideline chicks like

Mila or any of the others. To make matters worse, I called her a liar about being a doctor."

Niko laughed. "You're stupid. Man, that doesn't even compare to what your ass did. But I feel for you. Have you called her; explained your side; anything?"

"Funny, she said the same thing! But naw, man. I'm going to give her some space to calm down and try to see what happens from there. Thanks for coming over man to listen to my fuck up; I appreciate you, dog. Want a drink?"

"You're my boy; that's what we do; and of course, I want a drink. On another note, I'm going out with Sienna tomorrow. If there's one thing I've learned about dating friends, they talk about their problems so if the temperature is ice cold towards you, I'll let you know.

"Good looking out, Niko. I had no intentions of hurting her and I'm vibing with her, you know? She's one of those people who is genuine about her feelings and isn't afraid to express it. She knew we weren't a couple and was cool with it – even though I thought we could be."

"How could you think that still sticking your Johnson in and out of other folks on the regular? Man, you gotta put that thing in check. Some men love a thousand different women, but a real man knows how to love one woman a thousand different ways. That's what you've got to show Elyce. You have to make sure she knows nothing and no one else matters and find different ways to show her what she means to you."

"What the fuck? Who are you and what have you done with my boy? You're no different than me, Niko."

"I'm tired of that life, man. I want a woman who can love me unconditionally; beyond my faults and fulfill my needs. You could have had that with Elyce, but your desire to keep running your sideline hoes may leave your ass alone and lonely and guess with who?"

"My sideline hoes."

"No bruh, your momma! Who else is going to put up with your dumb shit?"

"You know what! Get your ass out my house. You way wrong for that one. But I appreciate your honesty."

"What about my drink though? Alright, man. I'll get at you tomorrow. Get some rest and figure out what your game plan is going to be to try and get your girl back."

8

"Hello."

"Elyce?"

"Yes, who is this?"

"The guy who's worrying about you making it home safely. What happened to you calling me?"

"Oh Lance, I'm sorry. Too much on my mind, I guess. Please forgive me. I made it safely and just crashed. I'm exhausted. Do you mind if I call you tomorrow? I wanna run something by you to see if you're interested."

"Hint?"

"No – surprise!"

"Fine. Good night, Ms. Lady. Sleep well."

"Thanks, you too."

As soon as Elyce hung up from Lance and started to drift off to sleep, her phone rang again.

"Hello?"

"Wake up, heifa! What you up to and why are you in the bed so early?"

“Damn, Sienna. I had a rough afternoon and I’m trying to sleep. Do you mind?

“Yes, I do mind. I’m going out with Niko, finally, and wanted to talk to you about it. Since you’re seeing his boy, I figured you could tell me something about him that I don’t know.”

“Was seeing his boy – that lying mofo. Not anymore – get the 411 from Jayce I’m too tired to talk about it. As for Niko, he seems like a cool dude. Go out, have fun but tell him not to be a liar like his boy and you’ll be fine.”

“Girl, what the hell happened?”

“I already said get that from Jayce and make sure you fill Lana in too. I don’t wanna re-hash that bullshit of a day that I had. Oh, it wasn’t all bad. There’s Lance but that’s a different conversation for later.”

“Fine, bitch. You continue to sulk over whatever the hell is bothering you but we will have this conversation. We have brunch planned tomorrow so bye with your stankin’ ass!”

Barely able to muster a laugh, Elyce managed to speak some words to her friend. “Bye, Sienna. Love you. Enjoy your date.”

“Well, hello, Sienna. You look great. Do I get a hug?”

“Sure!” She hugged him tightly and caressed his biceps in her release. “Thanks, Niko. So do you. I’m ready to go so you don’t have to wait.”

“Cool! Let’s hit it then. I picked out a new restaurant I’ve wanted to try so I hope it meets your approval. It’s the first step to us being on our way to a great time.”

Sienna was surprised to see a convertible white Lexus IS250 out front with the top down.

"Convertible, huh?"

"Do I need to put the top up? I know how ladies are about their hair!"

"Niko, I don't know what kind of stuck up, timid chicks you deal with but I'm good, babe. Got my shades, even though the sun is setting, the breeze will be blowing through my hair, and I'll be sitting beside a handsome guy."

Niko opened Sienna's, door making sure she knew that chivalry wasn't dead. He took the time to admire her sexiness as she slid into the soft leather interior in her sexy coral sundress that really made her green eyes sparkle nearly hypnotizing him. *Damn,* he thought to himself, *she was one fine, all-natural beauty,* noticing she only wore gloss to accent her lips.

"Buckle up, miss lady."

After a brief drive listening to some old school music, they pulled up to the Bistro in the city's historic district.

"Good choice, Niko. I've heard good things about this place. Can't wait to try it out."

"Well Sienna, it will be a first for the both of us. I hope it lives up to its fairly new reputation."

"Welcome to the Bistro. Dinner for two?" the hostess asked.

"Yes," Niko replied.

"First time dining with us?"

"Yes, it is, but we've both heard great things."

"Well, follow me. I'll seat you in a nice, cozy area," she stated as she walked towards the dining area. "Here are your menus. Your sever, Paige, will be right with you. Enjoy your meal."

Niko pulled out Sienna's chair taking the opportunity to peak at her backside while she eased into the seat already checking out the menu.

"Yum! The choices on the menu look so good; I don't know what I want," Sienna said excitedly. "Luckily I wore this loose dress! It looks good but there's room for my belly to grow after the delectable beat down I'm about to put on this food. Heck, I may need to pull out my cash now to pay for this."

"No way, lady! I asked you out and I pay regardless of how much you eat or the bill. Get what you like as long as you promise to have a good time."

"Don't worry; you won't have to tell me twice!" Sienna said laughing.

Just as they finished their chat about the menu, the server arrived.

"How are you all doing? My name is Paige and I'll be your server this evening. Would you like to start off with a beverage or appetizer?"

"Paige, is it?" Niko asked.

"Yes, that's correct."

"We're newbie's here – how's the food?"

"It's really good but my favorite dishes happen to be the char-broiled pork chops or the ribs. The kettle fried chips are one of our most popular appetizers too."

Sienna raised her hand signaling Paige to stop. "Ok, my mouth is starting to water. Let's start with the chips, calamari, and a pear martini.

"I'll keep it simple, Paige," Niko chimed in. "Please bring me glass of water and a vodka and cranberry."

"No problem, sir, miss. I'll be right back with your drinks and appetizers."

Hours passed as Sienna and Niko laughed and got to know each other. It seemed like they have been friends forever.

"Whew! Oh my goodness, Niko, I am so stuffed. This food was the absolute bomb. But I have to have some red velvet cake, too. What about you?"

"Naw, babe, I think I'll pass on dessert and have another drink. Just get an extra fork for me."

"I hope you enjoyed your meal. Did you leave room for dessert?" Paige asked.

"Yes, we absolutely did, Paige. Thank you. The lady will have the red velvet and I'll have a refill on my drink, an extra fork, and the bill."

"Sure, no problem, sir. Will there be anything else?"

"No!" They both responded, laughing at the coincidence.

"Where to after dessert, pretty lady? Feel like going home yet?"

"No way. I'm having too much fun to call it a night just yet."

"There's some jazz in the park tonight. Let's go check it out. Then, perhaps we can find a spot to get our dance groove on to work off some of this food, Sienna. What do you say to that?"

"There's that late night spot up 85. I can't think of the name, but I know how to get us there after the park," she replied.

The last performer was just coming on stage when

Sienna and Niko arrived.

"You still want to burn off some of that food later? I don't want your little feet hurting."

"Whatever, man! My shoes are very comfortable."

Niko grabbed Sienna's hand and gave it a gentle squeeze as they walked in silence listening to the music.

"Sienna, Sienna!" a voice called out.

"Babe, I think someone is calling you."

"Sienna!" the voice called again. "Over here, on the grass, girl!"

Sienna looked over and saw Jayce laid out on a blanket leaning on a guy she didn't quite recognize. She and Niko walked over to where they were.

"What's up girl?" Sienna asked. "Who's your friend? He looks familiar," she whispered in Jayce's ear.

"Girl, you remember Tariq."

"Oh shit – Lana's Tariq? She's going to beat your ass."

"We are both grown; Lana will be just fine. What

are you doing out here with Niko; Xavier's friend, right?"

"Yes, that's right. We met on the rooftop. Nice to see you again, Jayce."

"Hmmm, Sienna have you spoken to Elyce?

She's in a funk today." Jayce looked over at Niko. "I hope you're treating my girl better than your boy treated my other girl."

"Now, they're grown. I'm not going to get into it. I'm on a date with a beautiful woman having a great evening. I will not discuss anything outside of what's happening right here, this very moment and cause my evening to go downhill," Niko replied.

"My bad, Niko, you're right. Sienna, we will have a full discussion at brunch tomorrow. Tariq, you remember Sienna, right?"

"Yes. Hey there; nice to see you again."

"Likewise, Tariq. This is my friend, Niko."

The guys gave each other the customary greeting.

"Why don't you guys sit down and join us for this last set?" Tariq offered. "We've got some beer, wine and food."

"Niko, you don't mind if we hang out for a minute, do you? "

"Of course not. I'm going to pass on the food; we just ate a huge meal, but I will have that beer."

"Don't get too comfortable, son. You still owe me a dance or two, Niko." The foursome sat in silence enjoying the music. After a few songs, Sienna nudged Niko letting him know it was time to move on.

"Sienna, you don't have to leave, do you?" Jayce asked.

"No, girl. But I want to continue my single date – not embark on a double date; you feel me?"

"Yeah girl, I feel you but let me talk to you for a second. Come take a short walk with me."

The girls excused themselves and stepped away from the guys who've been chatting about sports and the carelessness of some athletes.

"Look, don't say anything to Lana. We haven't figured out how to tell her about us. I told Elyce but swore her to secrecy. Girl, I know he's young but very mature for his age. We have a great time together and the sex, OMG, is off the chain!"

"OK, Jayce. T.M.I. But I'm glad you're happy. Now, I'm going to get out of here so maybe me and Niko can have amazing sex too, someday; not today. Not going out like that on the first date. Now, let me get back to my date, lady."

'OK, fine I understand, Sienna. See you at brunch tomorrow."

"Niko, you ready to head to that place to work off this food?"

"Absolutely. Nice to see you both again. Enjoy the rest of your night," Niko said to Jayce and Tariq while taking Sienna's hand.

The pair made it to the club and immediately hit the dance floor trying to out dance each other.

"Sienna, you know you were doing your thing up in the club. Had me breaking a sweat and shit. I haven't done that since my days in college. Must be the company."

"Oh, it's definitely the company and the closeness of my ass in your crotch." She winked at Niko and gave him a tap on the butt after he helped her out of the car. "Thank you, again, for a great evening."

"I hope we can do this again, Sienna. How does tomorrow look for you?"

"Sorry, the girls have plans; plus, Elyce has that Xavier issue we need to discuss."

"Uh oh. That's my cue to leave," he said as he laughed and pulled her toward him. "I don't want to assume it's ok, so do you mind if I kiss you goodnight?"

Sienna didn't answer, she just leaned in and kissed him first.

"Does that answer your question, perfect gentleman?"

"Yes, it does." Niko kissed her again deeply saving a few for her forehead, neck and bare shoulders.

"Alright now, Niko! You better stop before this turns into you going home with blue balls."

"Ouch! I don't think I can handle that pain tonight. Let's touch base tomorrow and see if there's even a few hours for us to connect; maybe catch a movie or something."

"Well, I won't say no but these girls day out can go longer than planned. But I will call. Thanks again. Goodnight, Niko."

9

"Where the hell is Elyce? She is coming right?" Sienna questioned.

"As far as I know she is. I haven't spoken to her since yesterday. What about you, Lana?"

"No, Jayce. I haven't talked to her either. I just know what you told me about Xavier and that chick and some dude named Lance.

"Xavier? Chick? Lance? Wait, I think I'm missing some pieces of this conversation. What is going on?"

"She told me to give you and Lana the full details but since somebody had a date, I figured it could wait until we got together today."

"Oh yes, miss thang, how did your date with Niko go?" Lana leaned in for details.

"Let's save the conversation for everyone to hear at the same time. Oh, here she comes with those damn shades on. I hope her ass hasn't been crying all night," Jayce said with a smirk.

Easing her way into the seat Elyce removed her sunglasses with a slight puff to her eyes.

"Alright ladies, lets do this so I can keep it moving. I have some work to catch up on and appointments to reschedule. I'm taking a short trip to St. Croix. Anyone care to join me?"

"Let's see," Jayce chimed in. "I think I can clear my schedule for at least four days. You know I'm down. What about you, Lana?" Jayce was asking so she'd know whether or not she could bring her new man.

"Naw girl, I can't just roll out like that," Lana replied.

"Me either," Sienna added. "Beside, I'll probably have a date with Niko again this weekend. I'm trying to keep my composure before I have to attack that fine ass man. He gave me the cliff notes about you and X so what's the long version."

"There is no me and X. That's a wrap. I have to be the girl, not one of many girls and he obviously can't do that, at least not with me. So, his ass is in the wind and I'm on to the next one. He can go back to chick who was almost my hood ornament. I'm taking Lance with me to St. Croix."

"Hold up, Elyce. You just met him a few days ago. What do you know about this dude you're planning to take with us on a trip?

"What does Sienna know about Niko; or what do you know about whomever you're seeing Jayce and you too, Lana?"

"Wait a minute, heifa! I don't give a damn about who you're going on a trip with as long as your ass doesn't come back here with that fucked up attitude," Sienna said with annoyance. "Whomever Jayce, Lana or I am seeing is because that's what we want to do and whomever you're taking with you is because you're rebounding but what the fuck ever. Now that we've cleared the air with that ice breaker, let's order our food and drinks!"

"Lana, please order me a blueberry vodka and lemonade and I'm going to have the cashew chicken. I need to hit the little girls' room."

"Got you," Lana replied as Jayce walked off to the ladies room with her phone in hand. As soon as she knew she was out of earshot, Jayce called Tariq.

"Baby! Hey. How's lunch with the girls?" the sexy voice asked.

"It's cool. Elyce just said she's going to St. Croix for a few days and I'm tagging along. Can you get off for maybe five days Tariq?" Jayce crossed her fingers hoping his answer would be yes.

"Wait. You sure about me going with you? I mean, we talked about keeping this under wraps until we had a chance to tell my cousin."

"Well, until that time comes, I want to hit the beach with the man in my life. Elyce is taking a guy she just met, and I don't want to be a third wheel. This sneaking and creeping shit is taking a toll on me and I need to start letting the cat out of the bag with ease. So, are you in or not?" she asked.

"St. Croix! Hell yeah, I'm in!" Tariq exclaimed. "I'll get the details from you later tonight. Go enjoy your brunch, babe!"

"Cool. I miss you, Tariq. I can't wait to get your hot ass down on those sandy beaches. It's going to be on! Talk to you later. Smooches."

"Damn, Jayce, were you doing more than taking a leak or what?" Lana asked.

"Shut up. My bladder was full. What the hell are y'all talking about anyway?"

"I was telling them about Lance, Jayce," Elyce continued. "Girls, he was just what I needed after that scene with Xavier. He made me laugh when all I wanted to do was cry. He's a real sweetheart. I can't wait for you guys to meet him."

"Elyce, seriously, is this some sort of rebound? You don't even know this guy and you certainly aren't over Xavier. You sure about asking him to go with you to the island?" Lana questioned.

"He's cool about it. I talked to him and told him about my situation with Xavier and that I appreciated meeting him. I told him I was getting away and that it would be nice to have a friend there. He knows where I stand. If something happens or doesn't happen, it's fine either way. Besides, Lana, Jayce will be there with me, so I won' be completely alone. Everything will be fine," Elyce assured her skeptical friend. "Plus, you know it's my mom and dad's place. What fool would really get out of line with my father around?"

"Damn, your fine ass daddy is going to be there. Tell your mom to stay home!" Jayce joked.

"Please don't make me have to mess you up over my daddy, Jayce!"

"Don't make me have to fuck you up over your daddy! He is still one of the finest men on earth. He hasn't changed a bit in all these years. Damn!"

"You know, Jayce's right Elyce. We all think your daddy is fine as hell. Now our drinks are here, our food is here, let's toast to good friends, good times and great sex!" Lana said as she raised her glass. The four friends clinked their glasses and dug into their meals continuing to chit chat for what seemed like hours.

"Elyce, I really need to talk to you," the familiar voice said from behind.

"What the hell?" Elyce turned around to see Xavier standing beside her. "What do you want with your lying ass? Why the fuck are you here?"

"Xavier, you should go – we are in a public restaurant and really don't want a scene in here," Sienna spoke with a low tone while standing up.

"Sienna, I need to talk to her. We just need to sit down and talk. Shit – I messed up; I know that but damn, we haven't even had a chance to discuss it."

"I know Xavier, trust me, I know but give her a little time. Maybe she'll come around," Sienna pleaded as she grabbed him by the arm and walked towards the door.

"Please take your sorry, punk ass out of here before I throw something at you!"

"Elyce, sit your ass down," Lana sternly whispered in her ear. "You are not going to make an even bigger scene than necessary. Have you forgotten that you have a practice to run? You sure as hell don't want this to be the topic of conversation come Monday due to social media. Jayce, make sure Sienna gets Xavier's ass out of here right now."

Elyce was visibly shaken and tears were forming in her eyes.

"I can't believe his ass had the nerve to show up here, Lana."

"Just calm down and pull your emotional self together. He obviously wants to clear the air. Maybe, just maybe, you should give him that chance, Elyce."

"I'm too pissed and hurt right now, Lana. So that shit ain't happening. Maybe once I come back from St. Croix getting fucked really good by Lance—and believe me, that is the plan—we can talk!"

“Xavier, come on. Let’s step outside.”

“I’m not leaving until I talk to her, Sienna,” he said through clenched teeth.

“Yes, X. You are leaving and trust us, we know her much better than you do. If you don’t give her some space, you might as well wash whatever chance of reconciliation you have in mind down with the rest of the bullshit. Now, let’s fucking go right now.” Jayce pulled him by his other arm and led him out the door. Sienna and Jayce stood outside looking at the hurt on Xavier’s face. “What the hell were you thinking by coming here, Xavier? Don’t you know when a woman is pissed about being played or messed over, you can’t reason with her?”

“I wasn’t trying to play her, Sienna; I swear I wasn’t. I just didn’t think she would understand that I was trying to break things off with this other chick. I mean, Mila wasn’t my girlfriend or anything like that, but we’d had a long-term sexual relationship. I’m really feeling Elyce and want more with her.”

“If you wanted more with Elyce, dumbass, you shouldn’t have been fucking that chick that day – especially if you are trying to call it quits. That’s the problem with y’all. Pussy makes you even more stupid and it clouds your judgment.”

“Damn Jayce, you always gotta go so hard?”

“Fuck that, Sienna. Look, X! You messed up. Some—not all—women want the man she’s dating to tell her if he’s seeing other women and be a man about your shit. And more importantly, she wants her heart protected. If you can’t do that shit, then let her be. No one wants to be digging a dude and find out he’s digging you too, but digging out everybody else. Take your ass home, Xavier!”

“But I want to talk to…”

"What the hell did I just tell your ass?" Jayce snapped. "Are you listening? Please tell me there's a working brain in that head on your shoulders."

"She's right, X," Sienna interjected. "Please, just leave – nothing is going to get resolved with her right now. Maybe after she comes back."

"Comes back from where, Sienna? Where is she going?"

"Well, she's hurt, humiliated, been played, lied to, cheated on—need I go on? She needs to get away from you. And where is none of your business." Xavier sat on the bench outside the restaurant with his head in his hands feeling rejected and hating himself for his own stupidity. Jayce and Sienna stood there looking at him in disbelief.

"Xavier…you need to leave now!"

"You're right, ladies. I'm leaving but please tell her I want to talk to her as soon as she gets back, Sienna."

"Yeah…not! Don't call her," Jayce snapped with a huge dose of cynicism. "She'll call you if and when she's up to talking; whenever she feels like talking. Now, if you don't mind, Sienna and I need to get back inside."

The ladies stood at the door and watched Xavier walk towards the parking lot before heading back inside. As Sienna and Jayce approached the table, Elyce still hadn't managed to calm down.

"I hope y'all got rid of that liar. I can't believe he showed up here. I should have cut his ass."

"You don't mean that, Elyce. You're just hurt and angry and lashing out with words that you don't mean."

"Oh, I mean them, Sienna."

"No, your ass doesn't – whatever, heifa. Now can we get back to our food and our plans for the island?"

10

"Mom, Daddy?" Elyce called out. "We're here."

Elyce and her friends made it to her parents' house. The door was open, so she knew they hadn't relaxed that much to leave the doors unlocked and not be home – even on the island. There was dead silence inside the house.

"Now, where could they be?" Elyce asked the group but not really expecting an answer. "I just talked to them at the airport and told them we'd be here shortly."

"Hey, baby girl!" That's how Elyce's dad always referred to her unless she was in trouble. It always brought a smile to her face.

"Daddy! Hi. I was beginning to think you guys were ignoring me."

"Now would I do that to my favorite daughter?" Mr. Xavier asked as he squeezed his daughter in a long embrace.

"Quit playing, daddy! I'm your favorite because I'm your only. Where's mom?"

"Oh, she's out back chillin'." He pointed towards the patio. "She said you all are grown and she's not hand holding a bunch of grown folk. She figured you'd eventually find your way out to the pool."

Letting go of Elyce, he walked towards Jayce. "I see you brought one of my other favorite daughters."

"Hey, Papa Xavier. So good to see you again. This is my man, Tariq. Tariq, meet Mr. Xavier."

"Hello, sir." Tariq reached out to shake his hand. "Thank you for inviting me into your beautiful island home."

"Hmmm, I see this one has some manners, Jayce. Bout time! Nice to meet you, son."

"Dang, Papa X – why you gotta be frontin' on me like that?"

"You know I'm just playing a little," he chuckled. "And who are you, young man?" Mr. Xavier asked, looking across the countertop bar at the stranger on the other side.

"Daddy, this is my friend, Lance. He's going to be hanging out with us this week."

"Separate rooms, right?" Mr. Xavier asked as he held a death grip to Lance's arm and hand.

"Of course, sir." Lance's voice sounded somewhat nervous with his response.

"Daddy, quit foolin' around. I'm grown; Lance is my friend and we are not having separate rooms."

"Yeah, Papa X. That goes for me, too!

"Now, Elyce, if you and Jayce are so grown that you want to share a room with your guys and keep me and your mom up all night, you should have stayed in a hotel instead."

"Austin, stop harassing everyone and let them get settled in their rooms." Elyce's mom walked in holding a glass of iced tea, looking as gorgeous as ever.

"Uh oh, the boss lady has arrived. You're in trouble now, Papa X. Hey Mrs. X. Always a pleasure to see you. This island life is doing you good. You're just as fly as ever."

"I know, Jayce. It's the island air and way of life; full of relaxation and fun." She turned to Elyce after giving Jayce a hug. "Hi sweetie. How was your trip?"

"It was good, mom. Please meet Tariq and Lance. They're going to be staying with us this week."

"So I heard. Nice to meet both of you young men. And speaking of young, how old are you, Tariq?" Mrs. Xavier asked while holding Tariq's hand, never looking away from his face.

"Mom!"

"Mrs. X!" Both Elyce and Jayce said at the same time.

"Did I say something wrong?"

"No ma'am; not at all. Let's just say I'm younger but very, very mature." Mrs. Xavier looked over her reading glasses at Jayce and smiled before walking over toward Lance.

"Pleasure to meet you Mrs. Xavier, I'm Lance, Elyce's friend."

"Pleasure's all mine. Well, y'all go and get settled and come meet Austin and me outside. We've prepared some food and of course some drinks. Be advised though, you will not get this hospitality every day while you're here. Make yourselves at home and plan to do for yourself." Mrs. Xavier turned around, grabbed Mr. Xavier's hand and strolled back out of the patio door.

"Your parents are a trip, girl. They talk mad junk."

"I know, Jayce. They didn't scare you guys, did they? My dad is a jokester and mom just says what's on her mind and will be asking questions later. Don't feel compelled to answer them."

"It's all good! Right, Tariq?" Lance asked.

"Fo sho…it's all good. Now if ya'll don't mind, I'm going to grab our bags and go to the room with my lady and freshen up a bit. So which way, Elyce?"

"Aww, hell. We've been here ten minutes and you two are already starting something. Down the hall, last door on the left is your room Jayce and Tariq; the furthest away from the parents. Come on, Lance. Let's put our things up and get out there before my folks come looking for me."

"We'll be there in fifteen minutes." Jayce winked at Elyce.

"Make it twenty!" Tariq yelled as they walked down the marble floor hallway adorned with original paintings and some and family photos from Elyce's past to present.

"Your friends and parents are mad cool, babe. Thanks for inviting me on this trip with you."

"No, Lance. Thank you for coming on such short notice!"

"It's no problem. Just so you know, I'm here to get to know you; not trying to bed you or anything like that."

Those words milled around in Elyce's head for a minute and she looked at him and frowned.

"You're not trying to bed me? Well damn. You need to sleep in your own room then, Lance!"

"Whatever Elyce. Let's go outside. I'm starving and dinner smells delicious."

The back yard was beautifully landscaped with canopy trees that created just enough shade and sunlight. Tulips in various shades of yellow, red, violet, peach and white were scattered around the base of the porch. They gave off such a harmonious, relaxing scent. Just beyond the porch, near the edge of the back yard were his and her hammocks tied to the larger trees. Close enough to the edge of the cliff where you could see and hear the waves of the ocean beneath them.

"Mrs. Xavier, thank you for this delicious meal. The saltfish, yucca, kale salad and plantains were better than any restaurant back home."

"No need to thank me, Lance." She reached over and patted him on the hand. "It's what you do when you're retired and enjoying life. Did you guys have enough to eat and drink?"

"Yes, mom. We're good. I'm going to take the crew on a little ride around to scope out the scene and figure out what we're going to do for the next few days."

"Sounds like a plan, baby girl," Mr. Xavier added as he emerged back out in the yard with his sniffer full of cognac. He grabbed Elyce around her shoulders and gently squeezed her. "And when you get back, let's me and you figure out which day we are going to talk about the practice."

"OK, daddy. But it won't be in the next few days. I just want to relax and enjoy myself without thinking about what's happening back home. Now, let me get the keys to the jeep so I can show my friends around."

"Man, Elyce, your folks are so down to earth and I'm loving this place. Thanks for bringing me and my lady along; I can tell this is going to be a good week!"

"Sure is, baby," Jayce said, giving Tariq's thigh a gentle squeeze. "We've already got off to a good start."

"Geez, Jayce. Please spare me the audibles that lead to visuals."

"Damn, Elyce, loosen up a bit. You know you want your back cracked this week. Don't hate on me and my man. I'm sure Lance has something romantic or adventurous for you too. Right, Lance?"

Lance curled his upper lip giving it a sexy look and took Elyce's hand. "Well, I'm the type of person who likes to show and not tell. So, let Lance do Lance; I got this, y'all. Elyce is in good, capable, strong, back cracking hands."

That frown Elyce wore on her face earlier when Lance mentioned he wasn't trying to bed her just turned into biggest grin ever.

The cool winds and the island sounds made for a good, relaxing ride. Elyce took her friends into the city past the craft market, numerous restaurants and bars. It was as if they'd all been dropped in the middle of paradise. The atmosphere was one you could never find in Atlanta. As the sun began to set, they drove along the road next to the ocean.

"Babe, pull over for a second. Let's catch the sunset."

"Lance, we have plenty of time to watch the sunset."

Giving her hand a gentle squeeze, he turned to look at Elyce who was trying to drive and look back.

"You're right, we will have plenty of time to watch the sunset, but the first one together is always the best one. It's romantic." He looked back and winked at Jayce. "Don't you agree, Jayce & Tariq?"

"Ahhhh yeah…that sounds really good and sweet. Tariq and I are cool with it." They'd been all over each other from the moment they hopped inside the jeep. Snuggling, as much as the seatbelt would allow, kissing and holding hands. "Come on, E, stop the car and get with the program."

As island living would command, there were several blankets in the back of the jeep. The fella's grabbed them and their ladies' hands as they strolled down to a secluded area of the beach. Spreading the blankets out to where they were close, yet far enough from each other, the couples took a seat.

"Take a walk with me, Elyce?"

"Where to?"

"Doesn't matter as long as we're together."

Lance extended his hand to help Elyce to her feet. She looked absolutely radiant with her hair slicked back, showing the strong features of her cheekbones and sparkle in her eyes as the sun began to set in them.

"You two behave yourselves while we're gone," Elyce yelled as they walked away.

"Yeah right, girl. It's me, Jayce, we're talking about. Take your time coming back," she said as she proceeded to unzip Tariq's tan linen pants exposing the bulge she'd caused him to have the moment she'd caressed him as they approached the beach.

"Whoa babe, we're on the beach; right out in the open. What are you doing?" He pulled her hand from inside his pants.

"How many times are we going to be on the island for the first time? Relax, T. You keep watch while mama works her magic."

Before he could object, she damn near swallowed him whole. The heat from her mouth made him moan as she flicked the tip of his penis with her tongue while pushing him back on the blanket. Slowly and gently she sucked and licked and caressed his sack until he began to squirm while trying to keep from cumming all over the both of them. His dick was hard and throbbing; pre-cum oozing out of his tip. She pulled him up to a sitting position and straddled his lap, facing him. As she lifted her dress to prepare for his entrance, he could see she'd left her panties elsewhere. The Brazilian wax was perfectly done, leaving just a slither of thin hair on either side of her lips.

"She's ready for you baby, let me give her what she needs," Jayce purred into Tariq's ear as she nibbled on his lobe holding him around his neck with one hand while using the other to guide him inside her.

Her walls welcomed the thickness of his dick just as it did earlier in the day. Moving rhythmically together, their breaths became rapid, their movements faster. He could feel her tensing as she squeezed him harder. Just as they both exploded, the bright lights of a car approaching the area near them made them quickly pull themselves together.

"You're such a nasty girl; but I love it and I love you."

Jayce was stunned at the words she heard coming from Tariq. Thank goodness he was standing behind her and couldn't see her shocked facial expression. She hadn't expected that. After all, they were having a good time even though they'd been joined at the hip for a minute.

Rubbing his hands across her still erect nipples through her dress and on down to her waist and hips, he turned her to him, lifted her chin and kissed her deeply, passionately with a sense of urgency he hadn't felt before either.

"I understand completely if this has caught you by surprise; hell, I caught myself by surprise. But I don't want you to feel pressured to have a matching response. It just feels right, you feel right, and I want you to know this isn't just about the good times, Jayce."

"You're right. I am totally surprised. It's good to know how you feel. I guess that's what island pussy will do to you." Jayce smiled and kissed Tariq softly on his lips before burying her head in his chest and squeezing him so tight. She didn't have to say the words, not just yet. He knew her feelings were just as strong as his.

"Thanks again for letting me tag along on this trip, Elyce. I wanted to take this walk with you to let you know that I totally get that you're still caught up on this Xavier dude. That's why I said I wasn't trying to get down with you like some hit it and quit it. I want to get to know you and see where this could go.

"Are you real right now? There aren't many men who would be walking alone with a woman talking about what he doesn't want to do. I appreciate you being a gentleman and all Lance but…."

"No buts! Let's just enjoy this time together and see where things go. OK?"

"OK."

As they headed back to the area where they'd left their friends, the waves were rolling in higher and higher nearly getting them more wet than they expected.

"Hop on my back, lady; I know you're not trying to drive home with the bottom of your dress all wet."

Hesitating for a brief moment to ponder what Lance proposed, she cautiously stepped behind him.

"Are you sure about this? You aren't looking at no skinny chick; these thick thighs save lives." She let out a light giggle.

"Girl, if you don't get on!"

Doing as she was told, he wrapped her legs around him as they walked back to their blanket just enjoying the sounds of the moonlit ocean.

"Yo man, what's up with all this lovey dovey stuff? You're making me look bad, Tariq." Elyce and Lance returned from their sunset stroll.

"Me?" Tariq laughed. "I'm not the one carrying my lady down the beach on my back close to the water, so she doesn't get all wet from the waves, Lance!" Easing Elyce back down on the blanket they'd laid out earlier, he stretched out across it and laid his head in her lap.

"Did you enjoy our walk and talk, Elyce?"

"I truly did, Lance. Thank you for the conversation and sound advice."

"I'm sure I'll be kicking myself in the ass about it later."

Elyce softly caressed his face. "Yeah, I'm sure you will but let's make the most out of this time right now."

Jayce was starring at Elyce with a "what the fuck?" look on her face, but she was in her own element after her rendezvous with Tariq.

"Obviously we missed something, baby. Everything good with you two?"

"Yes, girl." Elyce waved her off with her quick hand gesture. "We got this; so, worry about who?"

"Your ass, heifa! Don't forget it was your state of mind that brought me and my boo to this island paradise. 'Preciate, ya!"

The foursome had some wonderful days and erotic nights – well at least Tariq and Jayce did. They were walking around like two star-crossed lovers who couldn't get enough of each other. But time was coming to a close sooner than they'd hoped. Lana and Sienna we're calling and texting them daily to get the scoop only to be told, *you should have come with us*!

"Good morning, mom." The faint sound of Elyce's voice startled her mother; she's not used to anyone being up in the house that time of morning besides her.

"Girl, what you doing out here so early in the morning. Do you know what time it is? Why aren't you sleeping?"

"I should be asking you the same question," Elyce said, giving her mom a quick kiss on the cheek.

"When your father has more than one nightcap, he snores me right out of the bedroom," she said with a soft giggle and a motherly hug noticing the troubled look on her daughter's face in the suns early glow. "What's wrong, baby? Is something wrong with Lance?"

"Oh mama, I wish it were Lance. He's so sweet and wonderful and a true gentleman. He'd probably be the perfect man, but I can't stop thinking about Xavier." Her mother didn't say a word, just looked out into the sun rising above the ocean as she held and squeezed her hand.

"I don't know what to do, mom. I mean, I like Lance and he likes me, but he knows my story; he knows all about Xavier – which I probably shouldn't have told him because that usually gives a man the motive to make that move while you're vulnerable and your heart is aching. But he's nothing like that. That night when we walked on the beach, he told me he knows I'm not ready to move on from Xavier and that I may want to make sure of my feelings before I get too involved with him."

Pausing with her eyes closed and her head on her mom's shoulder, they sat there in silence listening to the waves crash upon the rocks below.

"Baby, you know your business is your business. It sounds like Lance is a good guy." She could feel Elyce shaking her head confirming that statement. "I must admit, he's right though. Before you move forward, you have to make sure your heart and mind are in the right place. When it comes to love, a woman always wants to know, not guess, her worth or importance to her man. She wants, no baby, she *needs* to know that she's a priority, not an option. If you're still unsure of your feelings for Xavier, talk to him, see how it goes; see where your position is in that little thing protected behind his chest."

"But understand you could miss out on something better in the process," she heard a voice say behind her.

"Daddy. How long you been standing there?"

"Long enough. I was missing my bedmate." Elyce's dad leaned over and kissed his wife on the cheek.

"Austin, you weren't missing me or else you would have said something all that time you've been standing there. You're just being nosey."

"Of course I am, honey; but my two favorite ladies are sitting outside in the wee hours of the morning without me. Plus, it's my baby girl's last few hours before she and her friends head back home."

"Daddy, I'm going to miss you and mom when we leave! I hear what you're saying about Lance, and you're absolutely right. But, Mom's right too. I do have to figure out where my heart is about Xavier. I love you both. Thanks for being great parents and for opening up your home to my friends. Now, notice I didn't say me because where you live, I will always live."

"Baby girl, I love you, but you are indeed a visitor!"

"Oh, daddy."

11

"I'm exhausted! Thanks for coming along with me guys."

"Tariq and I had a blast, Elyce. Right, baby?"

"You don't have to answer that, Tariq; I think we all know, my parents included, that y'all had a blast, Jayce."

Lance tried to turn his head to hide the laughter he was trying to contain because the two of them both looked worn out.

"Help me get the luggage, T; you look like you need a little break from this awkward moment."

"Thanks, Lance. You already know I was trying to figure a way out of that convo, man."

The fella's unloaded the luggage and said their goodbyes. Jayce and Tariq pulled out of Elyce's driveway leaving them alone.

"Thanks for coming with me, Lance. I'm sure this wasn't your ideal trip but you were a perfect gentleman and friend when I definitely needed one."

"No problem, Ms. Xavier. I'm just glad that I had the chance to go and meet some new friends. Your parents are really great folks. And, on top of that, I had a chance to go someplace I've always wanted to go. As for spending time with you, I've always believed in building a foundation that starts with a friendship. So, if and when you're ready and we're both in the same place in our lives, let's meet at our favorite spot." Lance leaned in and kissed Elyce, squeezing her tightly. "Thanks, again for letting me tag along on this trip…it was amazing, just like you."

"Oh, you say that like this is it. Is it?" Elyce asked, standing there with a puzzled look on her face.

"No E, it's not. We are friends and we can go out and kick it and anytime you need me for whatever, I'm here for you. But you and I both know you have some unresolved issues and your heart is not in a place to make any decisions about moving forward or staying put. I just want you to know I recognize that. Now it's late, you're tired; I'm tired. We both need some rest."

Elyce gently rubbed Lance's face. "Why don't you stay here tonight?"

"Naw, I'm gonna leave because we've been gone a minute and I can't promise I'll be a good guy!" He had to chuckle at his statement and she laughed along with him.

"Ok, ok – I was trying to seduce you anyway! But you're right. If and when it happens, it will. Thanks, Lance. I'm so glad we're friends. Good night and be sure to text me and let me know you made it home."

Lance hugged Elyce again, tossed his bags in the back of his car and drove off with a simple horn toot. Elyce stood there in the driveway watching him as he drove away. *Damn! Where the hell is my bullet?*

Elyce was so tired, she left her bags beside the car in the garage and walked down the driveway to the mailbox.

"Hey baby…can I come in?"

Startled at the sound of his voice, Elyce jumped. "Shit, Xavier! What the fuck are you doing here, scaring me and shit! What the hell is wrong with you?"

"I'm sorry! I didn't mean to scare you. I missed you and I wanted to see you." He stepped closer to Elyce and reached for her hand. She quickly moved her hand and stepped back.

"Go home, Xavier."

"Elyce, please – let's talk at least."

She looked at him with tears forming in her eyes but quickly turned her head, so he wouldn't see them.

"There's nothing for us to talk about Xavier. You made your bed so lie in it! I've been gone for a week and…"

"Yeah, gone for a week to St. Croix with some mofo you just met! You whoring now?"

Angrily, she spun around and slapped Xavier so hard her hand was stinging. He stood there stunned; with his hands clenched tightly.

"I wish you would hit me…you'll never hit anyone else…ever!

"I love you Elyce, I would never hit you; please baby can we talk?"

Tears were streaming down her face.

"I'm tired Xavier and I don't want to talk tonight. I just want to sleep. Please go home. And not that it's any of your fucking business, but I didn't fuck Lance or anyone else while I was away. I needed friends to help me through a tough time – thanks to your punk ass – and he, Jayce, and Tariq were there for me."

"I'm sorry; I didn't mean that. I was out with Niko and Sienna and I don't know if it was out of spite or what, but I asked about you and she told me it was none of my business, but you'd moved on and went out of the country with some dude. She proceeded to showed him a picture of the four of you by the ocean and made sure I caught a glimpse too. All I could think about was how it should have been me. I fucked up babe, I know that. But please...."

"No, Xavier...go home!"

"I'm not leaving until we talk, Elyce."

"She said no man! Something wrong with your hearing?"

"Shit...Lance – where did you come from?"

"I left something in the car, so I came back. Looks like it's a good thing that I did."

"Look, man, this ain't your business. This is between me and my woman so get your shit and get the fuck on!"

Standing in between Lance and Xavier, Elyce was towered by both men. She pushed Xavier back so there was enough space between the two.

"Xavier, who the hell do you think you are telling someone else to leave when I've asked you to leave?"

"We need to talk, Elyce!"

"We will talk but when I'm ready, not because your ass is feeling guilty about your shit and stalking me tonight. Now take your ass home or we'll never talk."

"Fine. You just remember what I said."

"Oh yeah, that you love me! You heart is obviously in conflict with your dick who must hate me because it seems to have other plans!"

Xavier's eye's widened but he couldn't find any words to say. He decided it was time for him to leave because this wasn't going the way he'd anticipated.

"Elyce, I'm sorry for hurting you." With that, he walked to his car, got in and sped away.

Lance walked up behind Elyce and held her tight. He turned her around and couldn't help but notice how her face was covered in tears. He gently wiped them away and kissed her cheek.

"Come on, miss lady. Let me get you inside and settled."

"I'm so tired; this day has drained me. I just want to shower and go to bed."

"You do that. Just point me in the direction of the bathroom and I will grab what I left and let myself out."

"It's just down the hall on the right. But don't you dare leave without saying goodbye."

"Gotcha."

Elyce walked in her bedroom and dropped her purse, shoes and dress on the floor in a pathway that lead to the master bathroom. She turned on the shower as hot as she could stand it and got inside. The water felt great on her skin; she was so tense from that encounter with Xavier. Just thinking about it, she could feel the tears beginning to swell in her eyes. She tried to contain her emotions, but she soon began to whimper. The tap on the door startled her.

"Hey, you ok in there? I'm about to leave."

"No, Lance, don't leave; come in here, please."

Slowly opening the double doors to the bathroom, he peaked around the door and didn't see Elyce. The shower was a slight way down from the door. Her fuchsia lace panties and bra were laying in the hallway just like her clothes in the bedroom, which he'd picked up when he came to tell her he was leaving. As he slowly approached the shower, he could feel the blood rushing to his penis. *Shit*, he thought to himself. This isn't a good look. Thankfully, the shower glass was partially frosted, and he could only see her shoulders and head which meant that was all she could see of him too. She smiled slightly.

"Thanks for being here tonight. Come take a shower with me."

"Umm, Elyce – you're upset and you're not thinking rationally."

"Don't talk, just listen and do…now take off your clothes and come inside."

Lance took off his clothes, opened the shower doors and slowly backed himself inside trying to hide his erect dick turning on the showerheads on the other side. The shower was large enough to fit four people, with double showerheads on each wall and a sitting area in the middle. Elyce walked up behind him and wrapped her arms around him from behind letting her hands travel down to his groin area.

"I think you want to be here as much as I need you here."

She stepped in front of him, looked down at his penis and let go. She moved over to the bench that had a small compartment from which she pulled out a condom. Tearing it open, she rolled it on Lance, grabbed his neck and kissed him passionately. He couldn't help but return the intensity of the kiss. He caressed her breast and ass as they continued to kiss, and the throbbing of his dick began to intensify. He wrapped his arms around her waist lifting her off the shower floor sitting on the bench with her straddling him.

Legs wide open and dangling on either side of his muscular thighs, she stroked his penis and guided his tip to her pulsing pussy that was eagerly awaiting the entrance. She pulled away from his mouth letting her head fall back releasing a heavy and sensual sigh. She rolled her hips moving as close to him as possible, so she could feel every inch of his dick. Holding her by the ass, he continued to thrust inside her but wanted to go deeper as he licked and teased her nipples with his tongue. Lance stood up and she wrapped her legs around him. He stepped out the shower, grabbed a towel holding it vertically on her back as he carried her to the bedroom, both of them dripping wet. Gently laying her across the king-sized bed with sheer curtains draped around all four sides.

She moaned sweetly as the weight of his body allowed him to penetrate her deeper. Their bodies thrust against each other harder and faster. He could feel her walls tightening around him causing the urge for him to cum increase. He couldn't hold back any longer; as he slowed down his pace to release, her breathing turned rapid and her eyes were tightly closed. She was cumming too.

"Damn it! Damn it! Damn it!" she screamed.

"Hey, hey, you ok?

"Yes," she responded breathless. "A week in St. Croix and it all comes back to Atlanta! Wow! Damn you for being a gentleman; I could've been getting my groove on like Jayce and Tariq."

"Yeah, whatever! You still have some unresolved issues and we've just crossed that *thin* line."

"I know. I'm sorry."

"No need to be sorry; just know that I recognize what just happened. Don't get me wrong, it was worth it but just like you, I'm not into being the option."

"I know that too, Lance. I needed and wanted that. I hope it doesn't put a cloud on our friendship or change what you said earlier. I dig you; you're cool people and I really want us to keep our friendship regardless of what happens next. Deal?"

"I guess. Well, I better go. You get some sleep and I'll talk to you soon."

12

"Welcome back, Dr. Xavier. I hope you had an awesome trip," the receptionist said.

"Thanks. Where is everybody?"

"Marie's in her office and I believe Lisa and Denise are in the back making sure we've got all the supplies for your surgeries later this week."

Elyce found it odd that her door was still closed; usually by the time she arrives, it's open with her day's work already in the center of her desk. When she opened the locked door, the scent from the various colors of beautiful tulips, her favorite, filled her office and flooded her nostrils.

"Marie," she called. "I know you know the answer, so come spill it." Marie came out of her office and looked at Elyce with a blank stare.

"Actually, doc, I don't but whatever somebody did, he must be very sorry. That's what all the cards say, 'sorry.' After the fifth delivery, heck, I stopped looking." Marie gave Elyce a slight smirk and walked back to her office.

Easing onto the chair behind her mahogany desk with silver accents, Elyce grabbed several of the cards from the flowers and faced the window overlooking the city. She began to read them aloud to herself hearing Xavier's voice in her head. I'm sorry; let's try again. I'm sorry; it's not what you think. I'm sorry; call me soon. Sorry, I miss you!

"I guess this must have been the last one to arrive."

"Who are you talking to, doc?"

Spinning around in her chair, Marie was standing there with a few folders in her hand.

"Myself, Marie – you know I do that sometimes; especially when you're driving me nuts."

"Well, I just wanted to bring you these files and your schedule. I've managed to stay on top of everything while you were away but there are always a few things that require your attention. When you finish daydreaming about Xavier or whomever, yell if you need me."

"I'll do that Marie. And for the record, you don't know everything, mom number two!"

Elyce stood by the edge of her desk and waited for Marie to leave so she could close the door and admire the flowers in peace.

"Yes, Sienna. A dozen tulips for every day that I've been gone."

"He's asking me, through Niko of course, to let you know how sorry he is and how he wants to start over. What are you going to do, girl? And what about Lance?"

"I slept with him!"

"Elyce! You did what? In St. Croix?"

"No girl, last night. But we both know that we crossed the line and it wasn't our intent and we don't want it to destroy our friendship. He knows I have some unresolved issues and we left it at that."

"So, what does that mean exactly? What about Xavier?" Sienna asked.

"What about his ass? How long had we been going out? You know the first thing I ask a dude is to be straight with me if he was seeing somebody basically from day one before we can even get close. How many ways can you let a man know you won't be an option if you're not the priority? Damn, Xavier!"

Sienna chuckled at her friend's rant. "You don't mean that, E; you like Xavier and you liked how you felt whenever you two were together. What about second chances?"

"I don't know. I need to think about it. Tell Niko I love him but stay out my damn business. Look chick, I gotta run but we need to get together soon. Come by later if you have a chance so we can finish this discussion."

"Will do. How about seven?"

"That'll work, Sienna. I'll order us something to eat too...Thai good for you?"

"Yes, ma'am, it certainly is. I'll bring the libation. See you at seven."

Elyce just made it in and was in the back changing her clothes when the doorbell rang.

"Just a minute, Sienna." She'd run to the door in her shorts and bra, swung it open without looking. "Xavier? What are you doing here?"

"Baby, we really need to talk and straighten this out."

"You can't just fuckin' show up at my house whenever you feel like it just because your ass is on the line, Xavier. You fucked her, fucked up, now get the fuck off my property. If and when I feel like talking to you, I'll call you."

"Elyce, come on. Don't let this keep lingering like this."

"You know what, you're right, Xavier. How about we get together on Sunday; I'll be sure I go to church and pray before I see you. Let's say 3:00 in the restaurant where we had our first date."

"Cool. I'll see you—"

Elyce slammed the door before he could even finish his sentence and walked away when the doorbell rang again. She swung the door open.

"Damn it, didn't I tell you—"

"Whoa, slow it down, sista! Don't be yellin' at me. Xavier is headed to his car. What was that about anyway? He barely said 'hello.'"

"He keeps telling me we need to talk, etc. I just finally said we could meet on Sunday after I get out of church."

Sienna closed the door behind her and walked into the kitchen while Elyce went back down the hallway to put on a shirt.

"You sure you're going to church?" Sienna yelled.

"Yes, I better go before I see him. You know I need help with this one. Why you ask?" Elyce said standing next to her while putting the food on the plates.

"Did you forget about Lana's surprise party for Tariq?

"Shoot, I totally did! My mind has been everywhere except on that party with these issues with Xavier and me sexing Lance." Elyce gazed out the window as if she was reminiscing about the night. "Damn girl, Lance put it down. I'm kinda mad he didn't make a move on me in St. Croix; such a gentleman."

"Girl, what do you really know about Lance?"

"Sometimes a stranger enters your life at the right time. I didn't know much about him, but I took a chance. Aren't y'all always saying I need to loosen up a bit? I know enough to know he's been a friend, a gentleman and that sex was good. Hell, I basically felt like being a hoe; I can get to know him later." She laughed as she and Sienna sat at the glass dinner table which was adorned with four of the flower vases Xavier sent her and one from Lance.

"Yes, you can be a little uptight sometimes but who are you and what have you done with my uptight friend?" Sienna grabbed Elyce giving her a sisterly hug.

"In all seriousness, we talked in St. Croix about work and life and why he's single – you know, looking for the right one, I guess. I'm keeping one eye open though. What man, who is seriously seeing someone, can bounce for a week in St. Croix like that? It's not that I'm torn, Sienna. I dig Xavier but..." Elyce's thoughts were disrupted by a loud bang on the door followed by a series of doorbell rings.

"What the hel!! This negro is about to piss me off!"

"You sit here, E. I'll get it and get rid of him."

The banging continued hard and non-stop startling them both. Sienna opened the door and Lana stormed past her throwing her purse on the chocolate chaise lounge. Her friends looked at each other and then at Lana who was pacing the floor.

"I just left Jayce's house and guess who answered the door shirtless? I know you two heifas knew about her and Tariq. Why in the hell didn't anyone tell me? And didn't I say not to mess with him any damn way!"

"What is your problem, girl?" Sienna asked. "So, now you know. They're happy together. Having a great time and all that and…."

"I don't give a shit!" Lana yelled at Sienna standing so close to her it looked as if she was ready to swing. "I said don't mess with him. I could kill Jayce."

"OK, Lana, what's the real deal about them seeing each other? We've all been friends for a long time; been through relationship ups and downs; the whole nine. Surely, it can't be their age difference. Hell, even you've dated a younger man who is obviously somebody's baby cousin!"

"This is different!" Lana screamed. "He's not my baby cousin." Tears began to form in Lana's eyes. "He's my son!"

"Oh shit," Sienna gasped. "What the hell do you mean he's your son?"

Lana sat down on the lounge with her head in her hands sobbing.

"I was 15. Smart in the books; stupid in relationships. I started seeing this guy who was several years older than me against my parents' wishes. He was real cute and told me how cute I was and how mature I was for my age. Clearly my maturity was in my shape and not my mind. I got so caught up in the things he kept telling me that I messed around and let him be my first…un-fucking-protected.

"I ended up pregnant and embarrassed. My folks sent me to live with family in Indiana until the baby was born and school was out. When I came back, the story was that my underage cousin had a baby and we were taking care of him because she was too young. My dad's sister couldn't afford to take care of the baby and raise her own kids, too. There was always speculation around my small town, but we stuck to the story."

"So, wait?" Elyce interjected. "Tariq doesn't know you're his mother?"

"No! And how in the hell would I tell him now? I can't believe J is sleeping with my baby."

"Sorry girl, but he is a very grown ass man or so we've heard," Sienna said laughing. Lana gave her the finger and silently mouthed the word "bitch" to her.

"Oh, Lana," Sienna came and sat next to her on the lounge putting one arm around her shoulder. "You kept that secret from us and we've known you forever. Now you're just going to have to deal with it, especially with his surprise party coming up. "

"That's right. That's when they were going to tell you they were seeing each other."

"Well, Elyce, I guess I'll have a surprise for them, too." Lana lowering her head in sadness.

13

"Hey Elyce, what's up?"

"Oh, Niko, I didn't know you were here. I was just stopping by on my way to the office for a few minutes to see Sienna. She here?"

"Yeah, she's in the back getting dressed. You know how slow she is. We're supposed to be going to get some food; a brotha is starving. Can I get you something to drink?"

"You know your way around the kitchen like you're living here. Something I need to know?"

"Naw, not at all. Well, yes there is but it can wait. Go on back and let her know you're here. Maybe she'll get moving a little faster."

"Maybe! I'll be right back so we can chat a bit. I want to talk to you anyway." Elyce's heels clicked on the hardwood floors as she walked down the hallway to Sienna's room.

"Hey girl, what are you doing here? Niko and I are going to brunch and I can't figure out what to wear. You want to come with?"

"No, mama; I'm good. I have to go by the office for a few hours before this party tonight."

"Girl, I'm so nervous about tonight. I've been avoiding talking to Jayce because I know I'd probably spill the beans."

"That's what I want to talk to you about. I'm not so sure we should let her walk into this situation blind-sided," Elyce said while watching Sienna continue to pull clothes out to wear.

"Yes, but it's not our place to tell Lana's very private business. You know?"

"I do know; it was just a thought. Guess we will have to see how it plays out. And girl, quit fooling around and pick something already. The purple sundress will look gorgeous on this beautiful day. I'm gonna go talk to Niko for a second. Hurry up!"

"Don't be in there grilling my man about Xavier! You ain't slick! Just call him already!"

"Whatever!" Elyce exclaimed. "Hey, Brother Niko, let me talk to you for a second; you mind?"

"Of course not, Elyce. You can ask me anything you want about Xavier."

"Oh, you think you know me huh? Well, here's the deal: I like Xavier, but I don't think I can trust him. I told him that night on the rooftop I'd prefer being told if he's seeing other women. He didn't."

"Women say that Elyce, but they don't really want to know the truth." Niko walked from inside the kitchen where he'd made a sandwich and sat down next to her on the other bar stool.

"Some women; maybe. But I wanted to know because what I didn't want is to be made a fool of and that's just what he did. I should have known from the incident with that girl the night we met that he was a player."

"He's not a player at all. He has never been into a woman like he is into you. Commitment wasn't his thing."

"No, commitment wasn't his thing, Niko. Having multiple women apparently is."

"Look, Elyce, was he dating or whatever when you two met? Yes. Were the relationships about anything serious? No. But when he met you, it was as if he'd become a different person. He was so excited about that fact that you were at the club that night. And once y'all started kickin' it, you were all he ever talked about. Hell, Max and I got sick of hearing your name – no offense." Elyce rolled her eyes and walked towards the window.

"Then what in the world was he thinking sexing Mila?"

"I can't answer that question for you; but he can if you would just talk to him. Give him a chance to explain."

"Niko, really?

"Yes, doc! Really. I mean both of y'all had some things in your life that you weren't up front about."

"Hold the hell up! I know you're not talking about my job. That shit doesn't even measure up to him not telling me he was fucking somebody else."

"Hey baby, I'm ready and it sounds like you need to get saved." Sienna slid next to Niko and squeezed him from behind. "You do realize you're talking to one of the most stubborn people I know. Don't even try to paint a pretty picture when it comes to Xavier. It ain't happening."

Elyce took a sip of the bottled water Niko pulled out for her earlier, hoping it would bring her anger down a notch; after all, it wasn't him she needed to have this conversation with.

"I'm going to hit the road guys. Enjoy brunch and I'll see you both later on tonight."

"Elyce."

"Yes, Niko?"

"Don't be mad at me; just meet him tomorrow and talk, please."

Standing at the door, Elyce pursed her lips together giving Niko a smirk. "Maybe!"

14

"Hi, Lana – it's E. I'm doing a few things at the office. Call me on the cell if you need me to come a little earlier to help you get things set up."

Elyce hung up the phone; she needed to get some things done before her full week of work and scheduled procedures after vacation. She had to re-arrange appointments with the sudden visit to her parents. Shuffling through the upcoming cases on her desk, she could hear her phone vibrating but couldn't for the life of her figure out where it was.

"Damn it…it's probably Lana calling me back. Ugh! I hate when I do that."

"Doc, who you talking to?"

"Shit! Marie…you scared me. What in the world are you doing here?"

"Well, I was passing by and saw the light on and your car. Wanted to see if you needed anything before Monday."

"No ma'am. I'm just reviewing my cases and stuff. You go on and have a good weekend. And don't be trying to bill me for overtime!" Marie peered at Elyce over her glasses.

"I got all my overtime in while you were off gallivanting with your folks. And just how are Dr. & Mrs. Xavier?"

"They're great. Enjoying retirement and island life. You should go down there and visit. I'm sure they'd love to have you."

"I don't know about flying to no island. Plane might crash in the ocean."

"Marie, it's not going to do any such thing; I'm back and I flew. Stop making excuses. Just go; you deserve to get away. I'm going to call momma and daddy and tell them you're thinking about it."

"Thinking and going are two different things, sweet girl! Well, I'm off to play bridge with some of my girlfriends. Don't you stay here too long."

"How cute. You got a crew, Marie. I won't be long; I've got a thing tonight myself."

"Okay, doc. See you bright and early on Monday. You've got a lot of work to do."

The phone began buzzing again. Elyce still hadn't found it.

"Shit! Where is that damn phone!"

"Watch your language, young lady…I'm not gone yet."

"Sorry, Marie; I can't find my phone!" Elyce yelled out of her office.

"It's on top of your sweat jacket in your chair, doc. See ya!"

"Bye, Marie. Thank you!" Elyce ran over to the chair to grab her phone. "Hello, hello? Darn. I missed it again."

Sliding back down behind her desk, she scrolled through her missed calls to see who is blowing her up on a Saturday. Xavier, two missed calls. Lance and Lana.

"I can't talk to Xavier right now," Elyce said to herself. She would call Lana first.

"Hey girl, what's up?"

"I'm so damn nervous about tonight! I don't think I can go through with this."

"Well, you don't really have to, especially not in front of everybody. This is a very personal situation, Lana, and tonight is supposed to be about celebrating Tariq on his birthday."

"I know but if I don't tell them now, who knows when I'll tell them. Y'all didn't tell Jayce, did you?"

"No! It's been killing me not to but, like Sienna said, it's really not our business to tell; just like them hooking up wasn't our business to tell you. But promise me this."

"What's that?"

"Please wait until everyone leaves. Tell them you need them to stay and help you clean up or something. Sienna and I will stay there with you if you need us."

"You're probably right. I'll think it over. Now what time are you getting here? I need you by seven."

"Damn, girl! You really know how to give a sista time to get beautiful. I'll go by the house, shower and bring my stuff over there to get dressed. See you at seven."

Elyce grabbed the rest of her cases and put them in her briefcase to review tomorrow. She clicked off the office lights, set the alarm and left the office. On her way home to shower and get her stuff for the party, she gave Xavier a call.

"Hello, beautiful."

"What do you need, Xavier? We're still on for tomorrow."

"I just wanted to make sure you didn't change your mind, Elyce. I'm so looking forward to seeing you. I've missed you."

"OK, Xavier; enough with the beautiful and the miss you stuff. If that's all you needed, I have to go. I'm kinda in a hurry I have plans tonight."

"Oh! With that dude?"

"I don't really think that is any of your business, Xavier."

"My bad! You're right; it's not my business but enlighten me anyway."

"I'll pass on that. Goodbye, Xavier. I'll see you tomorrow."

"Cool. Enjoy your night with ol' dude." Elyce could hear the agitation in his voice but so what!

"Whatever Xavier. Bye." Elyce hung up and held the phone in her hand for a minute thinking about Xavier. She'd actually missed him but couldn't let him know that. Not today, not tomorrow, not ever. Unfortunately, for him, she is still upset about the situation. Elyce was startled from her thoughts when her phone rang.

"Lance, hi. I was just about to call you back."

"Oh really? You sure about that. I only called you three hours ago."

"I know. I'm so sorry. I went to the office to catch up on my cases before Monday. I'm still so behind from our trip."

"Is that all you're behind in?"

"What are you asking exactly, mister?" Elyce could feel herself grinning widely with a memory of their night of passion.

"Well, we had a moment. A nice moment and we hadn't had one since."

"Well damn, wasn't that just a few days ago. Geez! What are you, a sexaholic? Oh my god – you're not, are you?" Lance couldn't help but laugh at her question.

"No, I'm not a sexaholic. However, I do enjoy good sex and that's what I had with you – that one time. When's my repeat performance?" The thought of him wanting to have sex again made Elyce wet while she drove, trying to maintain her cool.

"I don't really know about that, Lance. Don't get me wrong but you know my head wasn't really there that night. I don't want to sound like I used you but—"

"But you did, right? It's cool, Elyce. We are two adults and I knew exactly what was going on with you from the very first time we met, remember? However, if you change your mind, just let me know. Don't take too long – you know I'm a hot commodity."

"I just bet that you are. By the way, you are coming to the party for Tariq tonight, right?" Elyce pulled up into her driveway staying inside the car to finish her conversation.

"Well, I wasn't officially invited."

"Consider yourself invited and maybe, just maybe, we can continue that earlier conversation. I'm home now; gotta jump in the shower and get over to Lana's to help her get ready for tonight. I'll text you the address, ok?"

"Sure thing. Looking forward to seeing you tonight!"

"Me, too. Bye, Lance."

15

The guests were arriving and Elyce was trying to be hostess and counselor at the same time, going back and forth between the front and back of the house where Lana was getting ready.

"Tariq is going to hate me. I just know it!" Lana nervously paced back and forth across the glossy charcoal tile in her spacious bathroom as Elyce sat watching her.

"He won't hate you Lana; he may have lots of questions, but you'll just tell him the same thing you told us about being young and, well, dumb!"

Lana sat down next to Elyce looking a complete mess. "Geez, thanks, friend. That's real comforting."

"Seriously though, I really don't think the night of his party, in front of friends and family and some strangers, is the appropriate time to tell them, Lana. It's a personal issue and not everyone else's business. I know I've said this before but it's just my opinion."

"Now, we know opinions are like assholes and everybody has one, Elyce. I just can't hold on to this any longer, especially with the fact that he's dating my girl who knew he was off limits and didn't say a word."

“Come on, that’s not fair for you to be pissed at Jayce for dating him.” Elyce stood up and walked towards the bathroom door. “Who were you back when they met other than his cousin? That doesn’t give you any right to dictate who sees whom especially since we didn’t know the truth. Really, it could have been any one of us; it just so happens to be Jayce. Now, they are a couple and want you to share in that. You know she’s not going to do him wrong. Get out your damn feelings!”

“I know that, it’s just that my girl is dating my son and that’s just awkward. I could be her damn mother-in-law one day.”

“Look at it this way, because y’all are friends, she won’t get mad when you call her a bitch to her face instead of behind her back, as most mother-in-laws do!”

They both laughed at that statement knowing it to be true from some of their married friends. Just as the laughter began to die down, the doorbell rang.

“Finish getting yourself together and seriously, think about if you’re really going to make a mockery of this night by telling them your little secret instead of just celebrating your son’s birthday.”

Before Lana could respond to Elyce’s statement, she was already out of the bathroom door heading towards the front door. Elyce couldn’t see who was through the decorative glass that adorned Lana’s door but it’s a party! When she opened the door, the first person she noticed was Xavier. She tried to keep the smile from disappearing from her face but was a little difficult.

“Hi, Elyce. I know you’re surprised to see me, but I was invited to this lil’ shin dig by a bank client of mine. She thought it would be a good idea for me to come out and meet some nice women. Give me a quick second, I’ll introduce you to her.”

Unable to say anything but "ok", she watched him as he walked away in his dark jeans that hung just perfectly on him along with a crisp white shirt that was unbuttoned just enough to see a partial view of his pecks and those black loafers on that size 13 foot. *Shit, am I drooling at the mouth*, she thought to herself as she continued to inhale the cologne he was wearing as it lingered in the air? She heard someone talking to her, but she couldn't break her fixated trance on Xavier.

"Elyce, Elyce!" Sienna finally shook her by the arm.

"Hey, Sienna girl, I'm sorry. I was thinking about something and totally went incoherent." The two friends hugged. Niko was right behind Sienna. He reached down and hugged Elyce too.

"Good to see you, Elyce, and it's clear from the direction of your eyes that you weren't thinking but looking at my boy! You know you still like X! Don't play."

"Shut up, Niko! Ain't nobody thinking about your lying ass friend," Elyce whispered that last part as she saw Xavier returning with a beautiful young woman. Her skin was like nighttime against the pale, yellow sundress she was wearing with the most awesome summer shoes in hues of yellow, red and orange.

"Elyce, this is my *client,* Mrs. Natasha Rothe. Natasha, this is Dr. Elyce Xavier."

"Nice to meet you, Elyce. I'm not sure why Xavier is being so formal; just call me Tasha." She extended her hand arms to give Elyce a hug. "Sorry, I'm a hugger at informal affairs. I like the fact that your last name and his first are the same."

"Nice to meet you as well; your outfit is everything!" Elyce responded as they released their brief embrace. "And yes, the names are a definite coincidence. So, how long have you been banking with Xavier?"

"We've been working together for the last 10 years. And he's always taken care of my finances and banking needs. I do a lot of international travel as a pilot, so I need to make sure my husband is not mismanaging my money." Natasha responded, noticing there was a slightly raised eyebrow on Elyce's face. "You did hear me say husband, right? One of these days, I'm going to introduce Xavier to Lance, my husband, as he's always asking why I'm so cool with my banker."

"Lance? Now that's a coincidence, my date's name is Lance, too." She managed to say as she was looking at the four-carat rock on her hand. "So, just out of curiosity, why haven't you introduced them to each other?"

"He's a little on the jealous side and doesn't really like me having male friends, especially not ones who'll call me with that rich baritone voice that just blasts through the phone."

"Oh, I see. Well, thanks for coming out this evening; I'm slacking on my hostess duties and looks like the birthday guy just arrived. I hope you enjoy yourself, Tasha. You too, Xavier."

Elyce slid back over to the door but could feel Xavier's eyes on her just as hers were on him and she was enjoying the moment, knowing he was history and her date would be arriving soon.

"Damn," Xavier said under his breath.

"What's that about?" Natasha asked.

"It's a long story; one I don't really want to get into right now."

"Well, you may want to take a little walk to the bathroom, looks like your friend in your pants was feeling the doctor and wants her to feel him."

Xavier looked down and noticed the bulge he felt in his pants was becoming visible. He spotted a half bath off to the corner of the house and made a mad dash before anyone else notices, especially Elyce. He couldn't let her see the effect she still had on him. Hell, she knows he still wants her; she's just mad still.

Finally, Tariq, the man of the hour arrived with Jayce. Both were dressed in white linen looking like they'd just stepped off the red carpet. He was in loose drawstring pants and shirt while she was in a high slit skirt and shirt.

"What's up, Jayce?" Lana greeted her friend with a side eye at the door. "You're babysitting tonight, I see."

"Really, Lana? Are you really going to show your ass the moment we walk in the door?"

"Yes, I really am! You know you ain't right for seeing Tariq!"

Tariq could see the tension between the two women he cared so much about and stepped between them.

"Hey cuz, come on now. This is a party, my party in fact, and the last thing we need here is your attitude. If it makes you feel any better, I pursued Jayce, not the other way around. You shouldn't have such fine friends!" Tariq wrapped his arms around Lana and gave her a huge hug and walked off with her towards the den to greet some of the other party guest.

"Alright Elyce and Sienna, what the hell is that shit all about?" Jayce asked the two who were standing in the foyer where the exchange took place. "I'm not going to deal with this shit from Lana tonight. It's not about her or her bullshit."

"Girl, you know Lana is still upset but hey, it is what it is. Come on in here, girl. Niko is here with me and Elyce's man, Xavier, is here too!"

"Go somewhere with that mess, Sienna! You know he is not my man and he's probably fucking that Natasha chick he came with."

"Say what now? Did you say he's with someone, Elyce?"

"I met her, Jayce. She is not his chick," Sienna chimed in. "Elyce is trippin' but she ain't foolin' nobody. She was eyeballing him so hard earlier, I had to shake her back into reality."

"What? Girl, stop!"

"OMG! Jayce, he was looking so damn fine; I think I got a little moist! Man, I do miss the things he used to do to me. But that was then, and this is now!"

All three of them laughed and went over to join the rest of the party goers.

Lana had the party catered by her favorite southern cuisine restaurant, Old Town Bistro, and the food was smelling so good; she was glad she ordered double.

"These greedy asses killed the appetizers and are smashing the food now. You'd think they hadn't eaten today. Can I get you anything else, greedy Tariq!"

"Naw cuz, I'm still licking my fingers from that fried fish, collard greens, and mac and cheese! I can't wait to get into that red velvet cake. It looks homemade too!"

"You know it is; nothing but the best for you!"

"I love you, Lana. You've always been there for me like a sister." Tariq placed his plate on the granite countertop and hugged her with all his might. Lana fought to hold back the tears that were trying to escape her eyes.

"I love you too. I have something to tell you though."

"Hold that thought, I need to find Jayce first. Come with me; I think it will put your mind at ease about us."

Lana walked behind Tariq as he held her hand making their way though the crowd to where Jayce was standing. Tariq leaned over and gave her a kiss and she responded with an affection Lana had never seen before. Maybe she was wrong about her friend dating her baby.

"Excuse me, may I have your attention please?" Tariq tried to say over the talking party-goes and the DJ. People continued to eat and chat it up.

"Hey, shut the hell up!" Jayce yelled as loud as she could. It suddenly went quiet all throughout the house. "There you go, baby, the floor is all yours." The eyes in the room were questioning her actions but Jayce didn't care; it was, after all, her man's birthday.

"I want to thank you all for coming out to celebrate my 30th birthday with me. It's great to have family and friends like my cousin and her partners who put this together, so I hope you all will get your drink and dance on because you're already enjoying the food! Support your local community businesses like Old Town Bistro since y'all like the food so much!"

"Restaurant cards are on the table in the foyer!" Lana chimed in. "Just wanted to get that out while folks are still listening. Go ahead, continue."

"Well on this special day, I also want to take the time to introduce you to my lady, Jayce. Come up here, babe."

The group applauded as Jayce made her way back over to Tariq after she yelled at them earlier. She could see Lana standing just out of Tariq's view with her arms folded and her mouth twisted. Jayce eased up to Tariq, gave him a quick peck on the lips and wrapped her arm behind him so that his was resting on her shoulder.

"This lovely woman is my lady. From the first time I laid eyes on her that evening on the rooftop while at work, I knew I had to have her. She was resistant at first. I think that had something to do with my cousin Lana trying to keep her friends away from me. But, I was persistent and made it my business to get her into my life on something real; not just some hit and quit. I love her for who she and what she has taught me over these last six months. Babe, thank you for being my rock." Tariq leaned over and kissed her like they were in the privacy of their own home. Jayce had to break away before they both got carried away.

"Excuse me, everyone," Lana chimed in. "Since we are making announcements, I have one I'd like to make to the happy couple as well—" Just like clockwork, the doorbell rang.

"Hey, Lana! Hold that thought," Elyce said. "Let me get the door. DJ, can you play a little something in the meantime?" Clearly trying to change the mood, hoping Lana would not embarrass Tariq. The DJ threw on a mellow groove party break music.

"That was super sweet, don't you think, Xavier?" Natasha said. He simply nodded in agreement. "I noticed you haven't taken your eyes off the doctor since we got here. Why don't you just undo whatever it is that you did?"

"Don't you think I've tried? She's just stubborn like most women but that doesn't mean I'm going to give up. She'll come around."

When Elyce answered the door, she was so happy it was Lance as things were starting to get a little weird with Jayce's sudden announcement.

"Oh, hell fuckin' no!"

"What's up, Tasha?" Xavier looked in the direction his friend was looking and saw Elyce over by the door hugging and kissing on the guy that walked in.

"Hey baby, I'm so happy you finally made it. My ex is here, and I was beginning to get a little uncomfortable. He's been sorta staring at me all night."

"Well I'm here now, Elyce. We'll just have to show him that you are no longer available or interested in him." Just as he leaned down to kiss Elyce again, Lance spotted, Natasha Rothe, his wife. He stopped dead in his tracks.

"Lance, what's wrong?" Elyce was puzzled by his sudden release of her and he looked as if he'd seen a ghost.

"What the fuck do you think you're doing, Lance?"

Elyce turned to see both Natasha and Xavier standing a short distance from them.

"Whoa, wait a minute, Natasha, what's going on?""I guess I could ask you the same damn thing, Elyce. Mutherfucka, you better say something right fucking now!"

"Um, hey babe?"

"'Hey, babe?'" Elyce's head snapped so hard she felt that little neck pain. "What the hell do you mean 'hey babe'? Please, tell me this isn't what it sounds like it is!"

"It absolutely fucking is," Nastasha said, slightly raising her voice and catching the attention of Tariq, Jayce and Lana. "That's Lance, my husband." Natasha moved right up to Lance's face and beside Elyce.

"Babe, what are you doing here? Let's go outside and talk; you're going to cause a scene."

"I knew your ass had some shit going on. You ain't shit but I'll tell you what, you might want to get to the house, pack your shit, and get the fuck out. I hope you've got room for him at your place, doc. You can have him."

"You have got to be shittin' me! Lance, you're married?" Lance was standing there looking like he wanted to run right out that door he'd just come in.

"Seriously, the time we've spent together; going to the island to hang out with my folks as a friend; comforting me over Xavier's ass; and finding your way to my bed and your punk ass is married. Give me a fuckin' break!"

"Elyce, I'm sorry. I never meant for you to find out."

Everyone was standing there in disbelief. Tariq stepped up to Lance shaking his head.

"Yo, man. Get the fuck out before you get fucked up!

"Tariq, look man. I surely didn't mean to disrupt your night."

Lance took his cue and exited the scene of devastation. Elyce tried to maintain her composure but there she stood embarrassed, looking at Natasha and Xavier.

"I'm so sorry, Natasha! I had no idea. I've already dealt with one cheating ass," she said, looking at Xavier in anger. "There's no way I would be dealing with a married man; no way in hell."

"I'm not trippin' on you, Elyce. Lance's ass is notorious for this bullshit. My job keeps me on the road and it's the perfect situation for his trysts. But thank you for inviting him. All I needed was for his shit to blow up in his face. I'm done and if you want him, you can have him. But let me say this, you'd be better off with Xavier. That bastard may have a baby on the way from another chick."

"I can assure you of one thing. It's not me!" Tears began to form in Elyce's eyes but before they dropped, she abruptly exited the foyer and walked back to Lana's bedroom.

"Fuckin show's over!" Tariq yelled. "DJ put some party music back on. Happy fucking birthday to me!"

"Tasha, you ok? We can leave if you like."

"Sorry, X. I hope I didn't mess up the party. Tariq seems like cool people and I didn't want to go there but sometimes you can't hold shit until you get home. Let your girl know I'm not holding it against her; I'm sure it was all on his lying ass. You stay and see if you can talk to Elyce; I'm sure she's totally embarrassed." Natasha waved to Tariq and mouthed "sorry."

"Let me walk you to the car at least," Xavier insisted.

"Thanks for coming, Natasha. It was nice to meet you." Tariq leaned over and hugged her gently. "Sorry for this bullshit that went down. Hit me up if you need some muscle for that busta."

"That's sweet. Thanks. But hey, it's your birthday and you and your girl's night. You take care of this. I can handle mine!"

Xavier and Natasha walked out to the driveway.

"Are you sure you're going to be ok, miss lady?

"Yeah, I got this. I don't need his ass; I'm top notch! It's his loss."

"You've been listening to hip hop again, I see."

"You know it. Now look, Xavier, please let your girl know it's all good but don't be surprised if he shows up at her place tonight looking for somewhere to stay cuz I'm straight kickin' his ass out tonight, not tomorrow or next week. Tonight!"

"I hear you. Hit me up Monday and we'll fix any banking needs you got in mind. In the meantime, I'll go ahead a put a hold on his access to your accounts when I get to my computer tonight."

"Always looking out for your clients! Thanks, Xavier. Enjoy the rest of your night."

Natasha hopped in her midnight blue Audi A8 and took off.

16

Jayce, Sienna and Lana were in the bedroom with Elyce while Tariq tried to keep the party going in their absence.

"I don't believe that muthafucka played me like that! I should have seen that shit coming. Just my damn luck when it comes to men. What the hell is wrong with me?"

"Really, Elyce!? I know you are not trying to make it seem as if there's something wrong with you. Girl, you are beautiful, successful and smart."

"Sienna is right," Jayce added as she handed her a tissue. "And for the record, there's a man here who is absolutely crazy about you and you know it. Yes, I know he messed up one time. But he wasn't married and y'all weren't in a monogamous relationship."

"Are you serious right now, J? Xavier is an ass and I don't think I can take deal with his lies."

"Now that's funny."

"What's funny about that Lana?"

"You can't deal with his lies, but do you recall that both of y'all were untruthful with each other in the beginning? Now, you won't say it but let's not forget that you told Lana you slept with your ex when you and Xavier first started seeing each other. What about that?"

"I needed some dick; our relationship was too new and he didn't know so whatever."

"But if he had, then what?"

"Shit, Lana, I don't damn know."

"Stop being an ass and talk to him like we've all been saying! Just talk to him, E! Please." Elyce sat on the edge of the bed still in disbelief and not really wanting to hear what her friends were saying.

"Elyce, I don't say anything to you because Niko says it's not our business. But every time they are around each other, he's always asking about you. And if I'm around, he's begging me to talk to you."

"I really don't want to hear this right now Sienna. You do realize I just found out the man I decided to take a chance with, introduced to my parents—even though we were just there as friends—is married."

"So, fucking what! Shit happens!" Jayce said with an exasperated sound in her voice. "Now pick up the damn pieces and move the fuck on! This is supposed to be a party. My man is out there trying to entertain a room full of folks and I need to get back to that."

"Speaking of your man, I need to talk to both of y'all."

"Really Lana, are you still going to be mad about me dating Tariq?"

"Well, after our talk maybe dating won't be an option."

"Wow! Really, bitch? What the hell does that mean?"

"No, Lana," Elyce interjected. "This is supposed to be a happy time for Tariq and Jayce; we've had enough damn drama for one night. Let it go—at least for tonight."

"Hey Tariq, sorry it took us so long to get back babe."

"Is Elyce ok?"

"She'll be fine. Where did everybody go?" Jayce scanned the room and saw Niko escorting the few lingering folks on out the door.

"Well, after you all went back into the bedroom, you know how folks just start talking about what happened and I don't get down like that. You're my girl and that's one of your best friends. I wasn't going to stand here and listen to them talk trash, so I told them to leave."

"Ah babe, thanks for having my girls' back. I know folks will be talking about this like it's front page news for ever."

The front door opened, and Xavier walked back in. Jayce and Tariq looked at him.

"Say man, what are you still doing here?"

"I just need Elyce to know that I had no idea about what happened, and I really want to check on her and see if there's anything I can do, Tariq."

"Xavier, I don't think you still being here is a good idea," Sienna added as she emerged from the bedroom and stood next to Niko.

"I hear you, but I rode with Tasha and sorta need a ride home."

"I'll take you," Elyce said as she entered the room. "We need to have a discussion about this fucked up evening."

"Ride at your own risk, my brotha!"

"Shut up, Niko!" The ladies all seemed to say in unison.

"I'm just saying. Elyce is pissed and she wants to drive my boy home whom she's also pissed at!"

"It's cool, bro. I'll take that chance because it may be the only chance I have to get her to talk to me."

“Suit yourself. You ready to go, Sienna?”

“Now, you know somebody has to stay here and help Lana clean up this place and it looks like it’s us, Niko.”

“Really, babe?”

“Yes, Niko, really! This is Tariq and Jayce’s night and clearly Elyce and Xavier need some time together so get to cleaning. Is that cool, Jayce?”

Jayce was sitting on the couch staring at the floor shaking her head as if she was in a trance.

“I’m your mother!”

“Oh shit,” Elyce said, barely audible to everyone except Xavier.

“Who’s mother, Lana?” Jayce asked.

“His mother, Jayce! Tariq is my son; that’s really why I told y’all he was off limits.”

“Get the fuck outta here, cuz. What are you talking about?”

“You’re my son, not my cousin.”

“That’s real fucked up, cuz! You don’t want me to date your friend so you’re claiming to be my mom now? Let’s go, babe. I can’t stay here any longer.”

Jayce looked at Sienna and Elyce. “Is she for real?” They both shook their heads yes. “And y’all didn’t tell me?”

“Shit, Jayce! She just told me and Elyce. Surely you couldn’t expect us to come to you with that and she hadn’t even told Tariq.”

“Oh, my damn. That explains why your ass has been being such a bitch to me. Right, Lana?”

“I told y’all at the rooftop bar that he was off limits!”

Tariq inhaled deeply and walked over to Lana.

"I don't care who you are; you don't get to decide who I can be in a relationship with. Let's get the fuck out of here before I explode, babe." Tariq grabbed Jayce's hand and pulled her towards the door.

"That's really fucked up, Lana! Real fucked up. Some friend you are to keep a secret like that!"

Tariq gently pushed Jayce out the door and slammed it so hard, that beautiful stained glass shattered everywhere.

"All y'all get the fuck out! Now!" Lana yelled as she stormed back to her bedroom, slamming the door as well.

"Well damn!" Xavier said. "This is not how anyone expected this night to end. Come on Niko, let's find something to patch this door up with first."

"Y'all do that and me and Sienna will at least put this food away and come back tomorrow to clean up and get the window replaced. Let's hurry up and get this done before Lana comes back out here flipping on all of us for still being here! I'll still give you a ride home. This has been one hell of a day."

"Cool. Thanks, Elyce."

Elyce and Sienna headed toward the kitchen. "Niko, I hope you don't have any bullshit about to surface with Sienna. I don't think our friendship can stand another damn outburst!"

"Naw Elyce, we got nothing. Right, Niko?"

"Damn right! I got nothing, Sienna."

"Ok then. Let's put this work in post haste!"

17

Tariq and Jayce rode back to his place in silence. He sat in the passenger's seat looking out the window, but she could see the tears streaming down his face.

"Baby, I'm so sorry."

"Not now, Jayce. I just don't have the right words and I surely don't want to lash out at you out of anger. Just let me be."

Tears began to well up in Jayce's eyes as well. His pain was her pain, too. She and Lana had been friends for a very long time and for this to come to light in the manner that it did was unacceptable. She couldn't wait to call Sienna and Elyce, hoping they could help make sense of what happened tonight. Jayce pulled into the driveway of Tariq's place. He was still staring out the window almost as if he was in a trance.

"Tariq, you're home, baby."

"What?" Suddenly, Tariq snapped out of his sullen mood and looked around noticing he was outside of his house.

"This was some fucked up shit tonight, babe. I thought it was supposed to be about us, our family and our friends. How the fuck could Lana do this to us?"

"I'm sure she had her reasons."

"There's no excuse for her doing what she did. Tonight of all nights. She could have said something years ago. Why now?"

"Because one of her dear friends is dating her 'cousin slash son,'" he said in air quotes. "No, it wasn't the ideal time, but it is what it is." He turned to look at Jayce, took her hand in his and kissed it gently and lightly touched her face.

"I don't care what she is to me. I love you, Jayce and nothing and no one can ever change that."

"I love you too, baby. Now, you go on inside and think about your next move. I'll see you later."

Tariq let go of her hand, opened the door and got out. He put his hands in his pockets and started to walk towards the door. Suddenly, he turned around and headed back towards the driver's side. He opened the door and sat on the side, shifting the car into park. He ran his fingers through Jayce's hair and pulled her face to his and kissed her long and hard. He then kissed her neck and slowly let his free hand move down towards her breast, stroking her nipple until it was rock hard and showing through her blouse. He kissed her again before he suddenly stopped.

"Whoa, there's a lot of passion in that kiss, young man. You better get out of this car right now!" Tariq reached over and turned the car off and pulled the keys out of the ignition.

"I can't get inside my house, sweetie. This is my car, my keys, and I can't get in without them."

"Oh, yes. I guess you did come pick me up tonight. Well, go let yourself in and bring me back the keys, please. I'll be over in the morning, so we can talk."

"I don't think so, my lady. When I go inside, you'll be right there with me. I need you with me."

He stood up, extended his hand to help Jayce out the car. Her beautiful thigh was showing through the high slit in her skirt as she extended her leg out of the car grabbing her purse.

"You looked very beautiful tonight, baby. I'm sorry if I didn't tell you that earlier." Jayce looked up and her man and could see the pain in his eyes and the remnants of tears on his cheek. She wiped them away.

"You did tell me, sexy. You always tell me. It's one of the things I love about you. Even if I were in sweats and a t-shirt, you'd tell me."

She reached up and put her arms around his neck, traced his lips with her tongue where she could taste the saltiness of his tears before giving him a kiss. She closed the door, he pushed the lock button and they walked arm and arm up to the front door. Once inside, they didn't say a word but started walking down the hallway where a faint light was glowing from the bedroom. Halfway down the hallway Tariq stopped walking, turned to Jayce and backed her up against the wall.

He bent down on one knee and undid the lace up shoes Jayce was wearing taking her petite foot and placing it on his thigh stroking her calf and thigh before pulling off one shoe and then the other in the same fashion. Once she was standing barefoot, he reached inside the slit in her skit and nuzzled his nose right into the triangle of her panties. She stood there aroused but not saying a word as he slowly pulled at the sides of her thong.

"Open your legs a little bit baby."

She did as he asked, and he slid them down, caressing her ass in the process. She stepped out of them and watched as he tossed them aside before focusing his attention back to her pussy. He slid his hands back into her skirt where her legs were now slightly parted and ran his finger over her clit before inserting it ever so gently into her opening.

"Damn, baby, you're wet just the way I like it. I can barely contain my own excitement."

"Aren't we going to the bedroom?"

"Yes, but not right now," he whispered. "I'm hungry for you."

And with that, his tongue began to flicker across her clit slowly. He lifted her leg onto his shoulder and she placed her hand on his other shoulder to steady herself as he continued to lick and suck on her with more intensity.

"Take your blouse off," he murmured between the deep dives his tongue was taking in and out of her pussy.

Jayce's head was tilted back, and her hips were swaying in a circular motion as she could feel the excitement in her lower region. She unbuttoned her blouse and pulled the shell underneath over her head, exposing her breast. Tariq slid her leg back down to the floor and made his way to her breast sucking and squeezing them one at a time, back and forth, from left to right. When he stood completely upright, his erection had his pants sticking out like a tent.

Jayce untied his pants and they fell to the floor with a slight thud from something in the pocket and she followed his pants down to the floor taking his penis in her mouth with one hand on the shaft and the other fondling his balls as she sucked and stroked him. Before long, he exploded in her mouth, something he'd not done before. When he tried to pull away, she held him by his ass cheeks as he throbbed and released all he had inside her mouth.

"Damn, baby, my knees are about to buckle. I'm sorry for that."

"Don't be sorry, Tariq. A lot happened today and I'm sure you needed that."

"Shhhhh!" He placed his finger on her lips and pulled her up from the floor. Bending over to grab his pants, he dropped to one knee again and retrieved a small box out of his pants pocket. Looking up at her still topless but wearing her skirt and him bottomless but wearing his shirt, he opened the box exposing a two-carat square diamond ring trimmed with diamonds around the exquisite cut and down the band.

"Before everything went crazy tonight, I was hoping to make my birthday even more special by asking you to marry me. Will you marry me?"

"Oh my gosh, Tariq! That ring is beautiful. I don't know what to say right now with everything going on."

"I'm not concerned about everything, Jayce. I'm concerned about you loving me, me loving you and me wanting to make you my wife. Don't you believe in love at first sight? I knew there was something about you the night we met on. So again, will you marry me?"

"How could I say anything but yes to that?"

Tariq took Jayce's hand, placed the ring on her finger, dropped the box picked her up wrapping her legs around him and carried her to the bedroom kissing her as he walked. He eased her onto the bed, her legs still wrapped around him as she reached for his again erect penis guiding it straight to her wetness, filling her walls with all he had to give.

"Thanks for giving me a ride home, Elyce. I just want you to know that I really had no idea about my client being married to ol' dude."

"Sure, you didn't."

Elyce still had an attitude but she wasn't sure if she was mad or thankful to Xavier for exposing Lance and the fact that he was married. Maybe she was being too hard on Xavier. He'd been constantly trying to meet and talk with her.

"I'd been trying to meet with you because I'd seen him with a woman, a pregnant woman. Which has now been confirmed from what Tasha said but you wouldn't give me the time of day."

"I know, Xavier. I just couldn't deal with you after that chick at your house."

"Elyce, we were just getting to know each other. I was still seeing people as were you. We hadn't established that we were going to be exclusive."

"Wait a minute; what do you mean, 'as were you'?"

"Well, doc, I saw you out at the Rooftop Bar where we met all cuddled up with some dude the week before you were at my house. But because I knew we weren't exclusive, I didn't throw it in your face while you were browbeating me and calling me a liar and a cheat."

"Oh. Well, I guess that's that. We're both liars and cheaters."

"So, it's just that simple now? Before I was the scum of the earth but now that it's you too, we're in this together?" Xavier shook his head in disbelief at what Elyce was saying.

"Look, Xavier, I was just out with him and if you looked hard enough, he was cuddling me. I was actually telling him that I wasn't going to see him anymore because there was a guy that I was dating who I wanted to get to know better. Then, low and behold, that shit happened."

"Yes, it did happen but don't act all innocent like your weren't dealing with anybody." Elyce looked at Xavier as if he'd struck a nerve. She knew he had a point but didn't appreciate the fact that he'd called her out on it.

"Get out my car, Xavier."

"So, now you have an attitude and want to put me out? OK, it's cool. I'll get out but let's make a truce. Let's agree to start over. I'm not seeing anyone right now and I know there's one person that you're not seeing any longer. So, what do you say?"

"I don't know about all that yet, Xavier. I'm not convinced you can be trusted."

Well, look, I'm not going to beg you to start over. I've asked and that's all I can do. The ball is in your court. You have a good night and do me a favor and let me know you made it home safely."

Xavier got out of the car without saying another word and walked to his door where he waved goodbye to Elyce and went inside. He could see the headlights from her car still shining through the window; she was still sitting in the driveway. Suddenly, he felt his phone vibrate in his pants pocket. He reached in to retrieve it and saw that she was calling him.

"Hello."

"Hi, Xavier."

"What's up, beautiful?" She hated when he called her that but knew it was just a term of endearment and didn't want to start another disagreement.

"I'm sorry, Xavier."

"Sorry for what?"

"For everything. The way I've been acting; accusing you of doing dirt when my own backyard was dirty too and for being an all-around ass these last few weeks. Maybe we can start over and try this friendship again."

"Maybe? I guess that's better than no. Do me a favor."

"What's that?"

"Go home. Think about the possibilities of what our friendship could be, and you let me know when you're ready for us to start working things out. Deal?"

"Deal. Goodnight, Xavier. And thanks for your help cleaning up Lana's place. The girls and I will head over there first thing in the morning to finish and get everything back in order."

"Let me know if you need me. I'm happy to help, too."

"You might as well come because you know Sienna is going to have Niko with her. I'm sure he doesn't want to be there with a bunch of women."

"No problem. Just text me when you all get over there and I'll come through. Be safe and don't forget to let me know you made it. Goodnight."

"Goodnight, Xavier."

Just as Elyce was backing out of the driveway, her cell phone began to ring. It was Sienna. She clicked the Bluetooth button for her car.

"What's up, Sienna?"

"You tell me. It doesn't take that long to drop Xavier off and get home. You know our code: call when you arrive!"

"Well, I'm on my way home now. Xavier and I were talking. How about he saw me out with my ex a few weeks ago and never said anything."

"Girl, shut up! What did you say about that? Busted in your own shit."

"Whatever! I really didn't say anything. What could I say? I'd been acting like such an asshole to him and really giving it to him about being a liar and cheater when I was the pot calling the kettle black."

"We all told your ass to quit trippin' and talk to Xavier but no, you were being a bitch unnecessarily."

"You're right, Sienna!"

"What did you say? Did you just say that I was right? Damn, did something happen in the last hour you need to tell me about?"

"No, not at all. We talked briefly, and he basically let me know that he's not going to beg me to work things out. He might as well have said piss or get off the pot."

"And what did you say to that Elyce?"

"Well, after he left my ass sitting in the car feeling stupid, I called him and apologized. I told him it would be ok for us to try our friendship again, so we'll see. He's going to come over and help us clean up at Lana's tomorrow, so Niko won't have to be there alone with us."

"Niko will be happy to here that. Speaking of cleaning up, what the fuck was that shit tonight? Lana just really went in. Fucked up everybody's night; especially Tariq and Jayce's. Lawd, how are we going to get this all back on track?"

"You know we can't fix this girl. Number one, we've got to let Tariq and Lana hash things out and hopefully that will bring her and Jayce back together. Right now, you and I are in the middle of a battle that is going to leave somebody happy or unhappy either way. And by the way, if you can't tell from my alarm blaring, I'm home."

"Alright, chick. Glad you made it. We'll pick up this conversation tomorrow. I'm sure Niko is waiting on me to get off the darn phone anyway."

"Damn right," Niko chimed in. "Bye, Elyce!"

"Well damn, was he all up in your ear or what?"

"No girl, I had the speaker phone on. I'll talk to you later."

"Alright, girl. Bye! Bye Niko!"

Elyce pushed the end button on her phone while turning off and setting her alarm back on. She kicked her shoes off in the hallway and left them; the plush carpet felt so good underneath her feet. She noticed the missed call and voicemail notifications on her cell. She plopped down in the chaise lounge and hit the play button.

"Hey girl, it's Lana. I'm tripping about this evening and you were right; I should have waited for a better time to air out this dirty family laundry. I hope he doesn't hate me for the rest of my life. Alrighty, I'll talk to you later. I didn't really want to talk, just to apologize for my behavior."

"Yeah, her ass should feel bad for what happened," Elyce said out loud. That was some unacceptable shit for sure.

The next message was a surprise.

"Hey, beautiful. Don't forget to let me know you made it. Thank you for giving me a second chance to show you that we can be friends and hopefully more. I'm going to show you just how serious I can be about the relationship if you just let me. Sweet dreams."

Elyce smiled at the message Xavier left for her. She sent him a text message.

Thanks! I'm home.

18

Elyce, Sienna, and Niko pulled into Lana's driveway at the same time. From the outside, everything looked great. Rose bushes in full bloom, nicely manicured lawn with spider grass lining the walkway. No one could ever have imagined the drama that took place in this house last night.

"Wus up, E?"

"Hey, Niko. Hey, Sienna girl. Y'all ready for this mess inside?"

"Hell naw! Who wants to spend their Sunday cleaning someone else's damn house? Not me! I needed to be in church praying that this all works out between Jayce, Tariq, & Lana and then let Niko take me out for brunch, right babe?"

"Brunch? I had my mouth set for some of your baked French toast. Nobody is taking your ass to brunch."

"You get on my nerves, Niko. You better be glad I like your stankin' ass or me and Elyce would leave you outside."

Sienna rang the doorbell as Niko stood behind her making faces and mouthing words he didn't really want her to hear or see. Elyce started laughing.

"What is his silly ass doing behind my back?"

"Nothing, Sienna." Elyce winked at Niko. "Quit being so paranoid."

Lana opened the door with puffy swollen eyes and a lack of sleep look on her face. There was sadness on her face as she looked past the three of us.

"Where's Tariq and Jayce?"

"What? What do you mean, 'where are they?' Did you expect them to be here or something?"

"Hell, Elyce, I wasn't expecting y'all, but here you stand! I called him last night and asked him to come over. I felt like we needed to talk, and I owed him the truth. I figured Jayce would come along for support."

Lana walked away from the group heading back towards the kitchen .

"Sorry to disappoint you. It's just me, Sienna, and Niko. We came to help clean up from last night and Xavier should be here shortly to help Niko fix the front door."

"Xavier?" Sienna and Niko both said at the same time.

"Oh, my sweet girl, Elyce. I guess there's something we need to talk about, girlfriend!" Sienna laughed.

"No, there's nothing to talk about. We are going to try and be friends and, as my friend, I asked him to come help sort out this mess. Thank you very much!"

"Humph; well, sorry to disappoint you. There's nothing to clean up. I couldn't sleep so between the tears from the mess I made, I cleaned up. The only thing left to do is the door. But I did cook breakfast because I was hoping Tariq would come. Clearly, he's not, so you're all welcome to eat." The doorbell rang just as Lana finished.

"I'll get the door. It's probably Xavier."

Elyce trotted off to the door while Sienna and Niko sat on the kitchen barstools looking at all the food Lana prepared. Bacon, chicken sausage, kielbasa, cheese grits, scrambled eggs, sweet potato pancakes, and baked French toast.

"Niko, it looks like you'll get some French toast this morning after all." Sienna gave Niko a quick kiss on the lips. Elyce walked back into the room with a smirk on her face and Xavier just steps behind her.

"Why do you have that look on your face? Morning, Xavier. Thanks for coming," Lana said as she walked over and gave him a hug. "It's really good to see you," she whispered in his ear. "Elyce is a stubborn ass like the rest of the crew; be patient." As she let go of her embrace with Xavier, her eyes filled with water as both Tariq and Jayce were standing at the entrance to the kitchen.

"Morning, everybody," Tariq said, breaking the silence that had engulfed the room.

"Hey, T. I'm didn't think you were going to come. I didn't know they were coming over, too."

"It's ok. I'm glad they're all here. Clearly, there's some talking that needs to take place and it might as well happen the same way it did last night. In front of everybody." Tariq gave Lana a sharp look, squeezed Jayce's hand and walked over to the spread of food. Lana hadn't said much of anything to anybody other than good morning.

"Since we're all here, let's eat, sit, and have a civilized conversation about last night," Sienna chimed in. "Babe, you want me to fix your plate?"

"Sure. You know what's primary for me. hat French toast!" Xavier looked at Elyce as if to see if she was going to offer to do the same.

"Naw, hell naw, buddy. Get yo ass up and fix your own plate!" Everybody except Niko and Lana proceeded to get their breakfast leaving the two of them alone.

"How you holding up today, Lana?"

"Niko, I'm afraid I've hurt the people I care about, you know. Jayce barely looked at me. And Tariq, I'm just not sure how this will all turn out."

"You've just got to have faith that everything will be fine. Could you have approached things differently, sure. But you didn't. It is what it is. You and them just have to pick up the pieces and move forward from today."

Lana gave Niko a week smile. He grabbed her hand giving it a squeeze to help reassure her that in the face of adversity, there's a light at the end of the tunnel.

"Here's your plate, babe." Sienna placed Niko's plate down in front of him full of French toast, eggs and bacon. "Now if that's not what you wanted, you'll have to go get the rest."

"This is perfect, babe." Niko gave Sienna a slight rub on her butt. "I'll show you later just how much I appreciate you."

Embarrassed he said that in front of everybody, Sienna started walking away. "You're so stupid; get on my nerves!"

"You know you like it. Stop trying to be all bougie in front of your friends. They all know about you, nasty girl!"

Elyce couldn't help but hear Niko and Sienna's exchange as her friend's face was showing the embarrassment.

"Alright you two, this is not your own little private room. Don't nobody want to hear all that this early in the morning. Messing up my damn appetite. Let's say grace. Xavier, why don't you do it?"

“Me?”

“Yes, you. Did I stutter, friend?”

“Naw, you didn’t stutter, friend.”

Xavier’s prayer was full of thanks for the food, the friendships around the table and for peaceful resolutions. It went a little longer than anticipated. Elyce was starting to regret the ask. The room was quiet as everyone ate their food; those first few bites were usually the time to savor the flavor and let the food hit your stomach.

“Lana, this food is the bomb!” Niko exclaimed.

“Yeah, what Niko said,” Xavier added. Tariq stood up and took his plate for a second helping.

“Yes, the food is delicious,” Tariq said, “But there’s clearly an elephant in the room and I’d like to clear the air as soon as possible.”

“Right here, right now?” Lana asked, looking at everyone in the room hoping someone would step in and suggest it not be done.

“Why not? This is family, right? These are people who are a lot closer to us than all the people who were here last night before you made a damned fool of yourself, right?”

“Tariq, that’s not fair.”

“What’s not fair, Elyce? I mean she embarrassed the shit out of me, been acting shitty with my girl, her best friend, and had it not been for your situation with Lance blowing up and me asking them to leave, everybody at the party would have known about a very personal matter. Please, don’t tell me about being fair.” Xavier looked at Elyce and shook his head giving her that look to say it’s not her battle to fight.

"Baby, just calm down. Come sit down and give Lana a chance to talk. Let's not jump to any conclusions." Jayce grabbed Tariq by his hand and pulled him back down next to her.

"Thanks, Jayce. I know you didn't do that for me, but thanks. Let me not drag this out any longer than I need to. Tariq, I'm sorry about last night. I let my emotions get the best of me and you're right; I made a fool out of myself. Elyce and Sienna pleaded with me not to make a scene, but I didn't listen and ruined your birthday."

"So, wait a minute, your girls knew about this but I didn't?" Tariq was getting agitated.

"It wasn't like I wanted to tell them before you, but I was so upset about you and Jayce and they couldn't understand why. We were having a conversation about it and they were telling me how happy the two of you were but all I could think about was telling them, all of them, you were off limits to them."

"Well, if he was off limits to us, to me, don't you think you should have given a better explanation, Lana? Hell, surely I would have viewed him a little differently had I known that. It would have been like dating my nephew. But instead, you kept it to yourself, he pursued me, and we are now in a relationship, a real one!"

"Jayce, I didn't know how to tell you, any of you! I mean everybody has secrets right? Everybody around this damn table has some secret or another whether y'all admit it or not. Anyway, Tariq, this isn't about everyone else, this is about you and me. To make a long story short, I was 15 and got pregnant. My folks thought it was better that you be raised by another family member and I would be your cousin. It was wrong to keep that secret from you, but it was what the family decided. I just couldn't bare the thought of my girl sleeping with my son. It's like your auntie and that's just incestuous."

"Incestuous? Really, Lana? You and Jayce are not family. There's no blood relation so that is just ridiculous. Furthermore, I'm a grown ass man and Jayce is a sexy grown ass woman. She's not like all these damn immature chicks I've dated over the years. She's good for me and I'm damn sure good for her. Whether you like it or not, mother or not, friend or not, she's my choice and it ain't shit you can do about it."

"Okay, okay. Let's not get the volume turned up here," Xavier chimed in. "I know I'm on the outside looking in here, but Lana has some valid reasons for not wanting the two of you together, albeit a little late. And Tariq and Jayce have valid reasons for wanting to be together. Lana, you know Jayce is a good person and, if her and Tariq are happy together, it's not your place to stop that."

"Hell, she can't stop shit. Not now or ever." Tariq was standing again anger in his eyes.

"Tariq, sit down!" Jayce tugged him more forcibly back into his seat.

"All I'm trying to say is they are apparently good for each other from what I've seen and whether you like it or not, it is what it is."

"I do understand that, Xavier! I just don't have to like it or approve of it."

"Whether you like it or not, this here, between Tariq and I, is real. So real he proposed to me last night." Jayce held up her hand and showed off the dazzling diamond ring Tariq gave her.

"Oh damn!" Sienna screamed. "Congratulations! That ring is beautiful."

"Yes, it is," Elyce added.

"I'm glad you two approve. Your dudes help me pick it out."

Elyce turned and looked at Xavier. “Why didn’t you tell me man?”

“Can’t tell somebody something when they’re not talking to you. Besides, it wasn’t my business to tell.”

Lana didn’t say anything while the others celebrated the news of the engagement. Instead, she got up from the table and went back to her bedroom and closed the door.

19

The food had been devoured but Elyce set aside a plate for Lana who hadn't eaten prior to going back to her room. The group figured she needed some time alone as it seemed she hadn't come around to Tariq and Jayce's relationship.

"So, Elyce, what's up with you and Xavier?"

"There's nothing up, Niko. Right, Xavier?"

"Sure, Elyce, whatever you say."

"Niko baby, I think there are some secrets floating round this room right now. Ain't nothing up? Not a single thing?"

"Hey, it's not by my choice. It's Elyce who wants to be friends. But as we sit around this table today, in front of all your friends—well almost all—I want you and them to know that I will show you my sincerity. Action speaks louder than words."

"Anywho! Why are we sitting here talking about me and Xavier? Jayce, let's talk about that sparkler on your hand."

"Oh, didn't really want to add fuel to the fire of what was already going on here, so we weren't trying to make a big deal out of the fact that Tariq and I got engaged." Without warning, there was a loud noise that came from the back room that disrupted the groups conversation.

“Did somebody fall? Did y’all hear that?”

“Yeah, Tariq, it sounded like a loud bump.”

Elyce was already walking towards Lana’s room to check on the noise Tariq and Xavier heard.

“Fuck!”

Elyce dropped to the floor where Lana was laying with her eyes rolling in the back of her head.

“Call an ambulance now! Right now. Lana, Lana, can you hear me?” Elyce checked her neck for a pulse. She found it slightly faint but there.

“Sienna, help me reposition her head to clear her airway in case her tongue is blocking it. Jayce, bring me a cold compress. I think she’s having a diabetic seizure.”

“Seizure? What do you mean diabetic seizure?”

“Baby, your mom—I mean, Lana is diabetic and when she doesn’t eat, she crashes. I’m guessing with all the drama from last night and not eating she probably collapsed.”

“Elyce, what can I do?”

Everyone could see the fear in Tariq’s eyes. He had no idea Lana was diabetic and, after all the things that transpired between them, he certainly didn’t want anything to happen to her especially with all their unresolved issues.

Xavier was standing by the door waiting for the paramedics who arrived in record time. He quickly showed them to the back of the room where everyone else was standing in the hallway while Elyce and Tariq were trying to keep Lana comfortable. The paramedics checked her vitals and immediately connected her to an intravenous drip. She was breathing but still unresponsive. Hoisted onto the gurney, the paramedics headed out the house with Lana. Tariq was right behind them.

"Go babe." Jayce gave him a quick kiss. "We'll be there right behind you. Don't worry; everything will be just fine." Tariq nervously shook is head as if he heard the words Jayce was saying but the meaning wasn't finding clarity in his mind. He jumped in the back of the ambulance with Lana and Elyce.

Xavier was standing by his truck. "We can all ride together if you want."

"I'll drive Tariq's car just in case we have to stay there a while."

"Jayce, you know we are not going to leave you and Tariq sitting at the hospital. Let's just take two cars. Niko and Xavier can leave if they need to and we'll stay as long as necessary." Sienna opened the door for her friend to get inside and ride with her and Niko.

When Lana awoke, the white walls surrounding her looked very unfamiliar. There was an IV in her arm and oxygen in her nose. What the hell was going on? Turning her head towards the door she saw Tariq sitting in the chair, asleep.

"Tariq," she managed to say through the dryness in her throat. He moved a little but didn't wake. "Tariq." She tried again struggling to sit herself up. Just as she did, Elyce walked in the door.

"Hey, hey girl. What are you doing? Lay your butt down right this second." Tariq woke up when he heard Elyce talking and jumped to his feet. He stood still for a moment, unable to move, not sure what to say.

She waved and smiled at him with as a tear ran down her cheek. It made him move closer to her. Sitting on the edge of her bed, he grabbed her hand, rubbing it gently and wiping the tear from her face.

"I'm going to give you guys a minute and let the fam know you're awake, Lana. Love you, girl! Be right back."

Mustering up a weak smile, Lana looked at Tariq and tried to sit herself up again.

"No, don't move or say anything," he commanded. "Let me speak. We're family, and I don't care how it is that we are related. Being family is all that matters. I love your girl, Jayce, and she loves me. We are getting married. I'd rather have your blessing than to not have you in my life going forward. We are all adults and we can come to some happy medium here."

Lana didn't respond with words right a way. She squeezed Tariq's hand as tight as she could and shook her head in agreement.

"I'm sorry," she said. "If you're happy, I should be ecstatic. Whatever you decide to do, I will support." Tariq hugged her as she let out a huge sigh of relief. "Family is all we have, blood or otherwise. Tell Jayce I'm sorry for everything."

Elyce, Sienna and Jayce came into the room and stood around Lana's bed. Jayce stood behind Tariq who was still sitting on the edge of her bed.

"Everything is cool. No need to rehash anything right now. We're glad Lana is finally awake. It seems this seizure made her come to her senses, babe," Tariq said. Jayce smiled at Lana and gave Tariq a kiss.

"Bitch, I'm glad you're going to get better cuz you were getting on my damned nerves with all this bullshit!

I love you and I love Tariq, too! I will not—no how, no way—call your ass mom. As far as I'm concerned, y'all are cousins!" Everybody laughed at Jayce's outburst. It was like old times with the four of them back together plus one.

"Looks like we've got ourselves a wedding to plan." Lana managed a smile through her grogginess.

As the ladies and Tariq were enjoying a good laugh, the hospital door to Lana's room opened and all everyone could see was a huge bouquet of flowers and the build of a man.

"Hope I'm not disturbing all the fun."

Everyone was waiting to see who it was because no one recognized that voice. As he got closer to the bed, Elyce got a side view of the mystery man and smiled.

"Hey, Max! What are you doing here?" Lana finally sat up in her bed and took a quick look at Sienna and whispered, "How do I look?"

"You look fine," Sienna whispered back to her. "But what do you care, you don't even know Max like that really."

"Hi Elyce, Sienna. What's up, Tariq? Good to see everybody. Hi, baby! Got here as fast as I could when I heard what happened. Sorry I missed the party yesterday, work life. How are you feeling?"

Everyone in the room was floored about Max's statement.

"Hold the hell up! Baby? Soon as you heard? Clearly, we have missed out on a whole hellava lot. Someone please explain." Elyce was looking around at everyone for an answer.

"So, we're all sitting in Lana's room and in walks Max. We're like, what the heck is he doing here and how did he know about Lana? Come to find out, they ran into each other at the gym and started talking, working out together and dating. And guess who he said told him about her being in the hospital?"

"Who, Elyce?"

"There must be an owl on this phone. I know you know it was you, Xavier! Man, why didn't you tell me about him and Lana?"

"I didn't know about him and Lana. Max is on the road a lot and he just happened to call me about us playing ball when he got back to town. He asked me what was going on around here and I told him about all the stuff that happened at the party since he wasn't there and how Lana passed out and had to be hospitalized. I thought it was a little strange that he suddenly got off the phone with me because we hadn't planned our ball outing."

"Oh, so you really didn't know?"

"I had no idea." Xavier shrugged his shoulders, hoping she'd actually believe him.

"Apparently they've been seeing each other for about several months. He was fussing at her at the hospital about not eating regularly. He was pretty upset about that."

"You know, out of our crew, Max is definitely the one who's more of a health fanatic. He's got a personal training business and that's what keeps him on the go so much. When you work with celebs, you can be called upon at the drop of a dime. Especially for those who've just had kids or need to drop pounds for a movie or tour."

"What? I didn't know Max had it going on like that."

"He's the shy type, Elyce. He's very humble and not one to put his success on the open market."

"I'm just glad he's here for Lana. Maybe he can get her in check this go around. I think this really scared her. Hell, it scared all of us."

"I'm sure it did. So, are we on for dinner tonight, doc?"

"Dinner? Are we going Dutch since we are just friends?"

"If that makes you happy, we can go Dutch or you can just pay for my meal and all my drinks too. Hell, you can pick me up and drive me as well."

"Real funny, Xavier. You know I'm just moving cautiously these days."

"Yes, I know. But I'm serious. Since you asked all those questions, you can take me out on a friendly dinner date. What you say?"

"Tell you what, let me facetime you after I see my last patient and we'll decide from there on who's going to take whom out to dinner, friend."

"Cool. I look forward to your call in a few hours. You can even approve my attire to ensure it's appropriate for our dinner destination."

Elyce leaned back in her office chair and looked out the window with a smile on her face. "He's trying! That's a good thing."

"Who are you talking to, Dr. Xavier?"

"Crap! Marie, you've got to stop sneaking up on me."

"Nobody's sneaking up on you. I just came by—like I always do on Thursday—to have you sign off on payroll, so I can get these people paid tonight. I don't want anybody looking at me sideways if their funds aren't direct deposited. Now, since you're in here talking to yourself, who are you talking about, Xavier?"

Elyce spun her chair around to her desk and folded her hands on top of it.

"Lady, you sure are nosey here lately. Don't you have some work to do?"

"I will do my work as soon as you give me what I need. Oh, and by the way, there's a huge bouquet of red and white roses sitting outside for you that say 'Happy Thursday, looking forward to dinner. Big hugs, X.' So, I'll just assume that you are in here talking to yourself about Xavier. He's a real nice young man." Elyce smiled and chuckled at Marie who was staring at her over the top of her glasses as she always does.

"When did the flowers come, Marie?"

"They came about five minutes ago. Xavier dropped them off to make sure you got them. He was on the phone at the time, so he was mouthing the words."

"What!? Five minutes ago? That sneaky man!

Let me have the payroll info, Marie. I'll bring it back to you before my next appointment. Thanks, ma'am! you can go now."

Hearing the sarcasm in Elyce's voice, she turned around on her heels and walked out of the office only to return right back with the most beautiful flowers. She sat them right in the middle of her desk.

"You might want to see this up close and personal just in case you're having any doubts about that young man's intentions."

"We are just friends, Marie!"

"Me and my husband of 34 years were just friends once, too! That's a good man, Elyce."

"You don't even know him."

"I know more than you think, missy! See ya!"

"Hey, wait. What do you mean you know more than I think?"

"See you when you bring me back those payroll papers. Your 4:00 has arrived early. It's a mole removal so you need to get your head in that game instead of asking me questions. Thanks, Dr. Xavier."

Marie walked out and closed Elyce's door. She shook her head at both the flowers, which were absolutely stunning, and Marie's last comment.

"I see somebody is making friends in my office! I'll have to have a little chat with him tonight." There she was, talking to herself, out loud, again.

Elyce took a quick look at the documents Marie had given her which was more of a formality and checking records because she knew it was under control. She signed off on the papers, grabbed her lab coat, smelled the flowers and headed to see her awaiting patient.

20

Elyce decided she would do the driving for her dinner with Xavier tonight. That way, if she had to bail early, she wouldn't be held hostage by the driver. She turned her charcoal gray car into the driveway and blew the horn two short times. After waiting a few minutes, she blew again, and Xavier came out the door, smiled that killer smile, looking like he's spent some time on his look and got inside the car.

"My mom told me never to leave the house when somebody blows the horn for them to come out!"

"I think all moms say that for their daughters, Xavier, not their sons."

"Is there a rule that says it can't be for men, too?"

"No but I'm just saying," Elyce said, smiling and rolling her eyes at the same time. "Where are we going, sir?"

"You just drive, and I'll tell you when to turn. It's a surprise."

Letting out a long and loud sigh, she told him, "I hate surprises Xavier. I'm sure you know that."

"Yeah, I do know that but so what! We are going out have dinner and I'm hoping we'll have a good time. Loosen up doc. Go with the flow for once."

Finally, they pulled up to very stylish art deco building that she wasn't familiar with. It had quaint seating outside with multi-colored tables, comfy looking chairs and umbrellas. The sign outside was blank still.

"What's this place Xavier? It must be brand new for them to not have a sign outside already."

"Just a little spot I came across one day. Thought it would be a nice place for us to talk and dine. I hope you'll like it."

Ever the gentleman, Xavier got out of the car, walked around to Elyce's side of the car, opened her door, extended his hand and helped her out.

"Thank you, sir."

"Forget what you heard, chivalry is not dead."

Once inside, Elyce really liked the ambience. Smoke walls with splashes of color throughout. Musical instruments and paintings adorned the place. High boys, tables, and booths with plush decorative pillows sat around the room along with a stage for a band and a fully stocked bar.

"We must be the first ones here. It's empty. I don't know about staying here. Let's grab a drink and go someplace else where people actually frequent."

"Relax, lady!" Escorting her to the far end of the restaurant. "There's no one here because tonight is just about me and you. I've secured the entire place just for our special evening. Now, if you don't mind, we can have a seat in this cozy corner booth and enjoy dinner and each other."

With trepidation, Elyce took a seat and slid towards the middle of the booth that was big enough for six people.

“Good evening, Mr. Tuft. Would you like your usual?”

“Yes, Germany, I would. And the lady will have a nice moscato, your very best in fact.”

“You’re funny, Mr. Tuft. Don’t you mean *your* very best?” Xavier gave his head a quick “no” head shake before Elyce could see him to the server. “Sure, my very best then.”

“Well, since you seem to be a regular to this no name place, what do you recommend I have to eat?”

“Let’s see, Elyce. I think I can arrange to get you anything you want.”

Germany returned with their drinks and a menu, handing it to Elyce. When she opened it, the name on the top of the menu read Second Chances but the pages were blank.

“Um, excuse me. Germany, is it?”

“Yes, ma’am.”

“There’s nothing on this menu, I think you grabbed the wrong one.”

“No, she didn’t grab the wrong menu. I wanted to be sure you saw the name of the place.”

“Yes, Xavier. I saw the name of the place. It’s Second Chances.”

“Yes, exactly. I would like a second chance with you to show you that I can be the man you need. The one you can count on and more importantly, the one you can trust.”

“Nice, Xavier. I believe you have my full attention.”

“Great. Here’s something for you.” Xavier handed Elyce an envelope. “I hope you’ll accept these things.”

“I absolutely love gifts!” Elyce squealed as she ripped open the envelop. A key slide out of the trifold. Elyce looked puzzled so she grabbed it off the table. When she unfolded the paperwork, it was an itinerary for a week in Anquilla at a swanky five-star hotel. The picture had the most amazing ocean view from a hotel suite.

“OK, Xavier, would you like to explain this?”

“Sure. I’ve planned a trip for us for an entire week. We leave one week from Saturday and I won’t take no for an answer.”

“I can’t go to Anguilla on Saturday. I have a full caseload next week.”

“No, you don’t. I’ve been working with my favorite office manager who has cleared your schedule to make this trip possible.”

“That darn Marie. I should have known she was up to something! Where is her loyalty?”

“Trust me, they are definitely with you. She was grilling me like you wouldn’t believe. She’s thinks of herself as your second mother and only wants the best for you.”

“OK. Fine. Sounds like that’s all been planned out. I’m always down for an island trip and the beach. So, what’s with the key?”

“The key is to my new restaurant, Second Chances. I want to make sure someone I trust has a key and can help me with hiring additional staff. Right now, I just have Germany, my bartender and chef who’s back there cooking up some awesomeness for us. Come on I’ll show you around.”

“Wait, did you just say your restaurant?

“Yes. My restaurant! You’re my first patron!”

“Ladies, welcome to Second Chances. I’m glad you all could meet me here today.”

"Wow, Elyce. This place is really nice. Xavier owns this?"

"Yes, Jayce. I was just as surprised as you are. Where's Sienna?"

"She's late as usual but I'm sure it's because she's going to pick up Lana. She's not doing a whole lot of driving since her hospital stint."

"Right, right. So, how are things between her and Tariq?"

"They're working on things one day at a time and that's great for them. She and I are still a little awkward, but I think it's just going to take some time."

"That's good to hear. How are you and Tariq?"

"We are so good; in fact, we are great. Girl, after Lana was rushed to the hospital, I thought he was going to lose it. He was stuck to me like glue for days. Good thing I'm my own boss. He was emotionally distraught from everything that happened. But when I tell you he made love to me like he was never going to see me again, lawd have mercy!

"We barely made it out of the hospital parking lot. I was trying to drive and his hands were everywhere except on him. It was off the chain. From the garage, to the hallway, every room in the house, you best believe we were in there. You know my ass ain't no spring chicken. The more we made love, the harder he cried."

"Oh girl, really? That's crazy."

"Yes, it was!"

Sienna and Lana came in the door just as Jayce finished. Elyce waved them over to the booth they were sitting in. The ladies all hugged and exchanged pleasantries.

"You're looking good, Lana."

"Thanks, Elyce. I'm feeling much better and of course Max is taking great care of me."

"Yes, Max. Your secret lover. We'll have to circle back to that conversation in a minute. I've got something I need to discuss with you all."

"Can I get you ladies something to drink?" Germany interrupted.

"Hi, Germany, yes please. Can you bring us some water and whatever they would like to drink?"

"Sure, Ms. Xavier," Germany snickered. She got a kick out of her boss and Elyce having the same name.

"Here are some menus as well ladies."

Germany took everyone's drink order and surprisingly, no one was drinking alcohol.

"Thanks, ladies. I'll be right back with your beverages and to take your order."

"She's cute, Elyce. Looks like she's barely 21. Is she one of Xavier's girls?"

"No, Lana. Actually, she's his 25-year-old cousin. But you know what, we are actually starting over, and I do not want to go into this with any doubts or pretenses about him. Not this time."

"Hey chick, if it works for you, it works for us."

"Thanks, Jayce. Anywho, I called you all here because when Xavier brought me here last week, he gave me an itinerary for a week-long trip with him to Anguilla. I've been trying to come up with every excuse imaginable not to go. I just don't want it to be too much too soon after everything that's happened. What do y'all think?"

"Elyce, why are you asking us? This is your life, your relationship or friendship or whatever it is your calling it. Personally, I don't feel like I need to validate your decision to go or not go."

"Sienna is right, girl. All I can tell you is regardless of what has happened in the past, a clean slate is a clean slate. If you're starting over with Xavier, start over. Start fresh and take your ass on the damn trip. I'm not suggesting you go; I'm telling you to go. You never know what you will discover if you close the door before it's completely opened. If I'd closed the door on Tariq— sorry Lana—I wouldn't be wearing this sparkler right here."

Jayce held up her hand, so they could get another look at the engagement ring she was wearing. All the ladies laughed at Jayce's last statement. When the food arrived, they decided they would each try a little of each others' meals because everything looked absolutely delicious.

"Germany, can you ask Chef to come out?"

"Sure thing. I'll go ask him for you."

"I think you ladies would like to meet the man who made all of this fabulous food."

Out of the kitchen walks this tall man, 6'5" at least with the most gorgeous salt and pepper hair and goatee. As he got closer to the table, Sienna squeezed Elyce's leg under the table.

"Ouch! What are you doing?" Elyce asked through clenched teeth.

"Hello Elyce, ladies. Welcome to *Second Chances*. I hope you enjoy the food today."

"Hi, Chef! These are my girls, Jayce, Sienna, and Lana."

"Pleased to meet all of you. I'm surprised to see you here without Xavier, Elyce."

"Um, I can come eat here without him, Chef. What are you trying to say?"

"Not saying anything at all. Ladies, I've got to get back to the food. If you need anything else, please let me know."

"Thanks, Chef," Sienna said in a sultry voice.

"Excuse you, ma'am. Don't you have a man? I'm sure Niko would not appreciate you being flirtatious with Chef!"

"He's fine as hell. How old is he? I need to introduce him to my mom or auntie or something."

"He already has a woman, Sienna. In fact, she's back there doing the desserts. And just so you know, Xavier has kept it in the family. That's his uncle, Germany's dad."

"A family full of fine. If that's what Xavier is going to look like when he gets to be that age, you'd better watch out. I may have to steal your man! Oh wait, he's not your man so technically he's up for grabs."

"Ha ha, very funny, Lana. Like the old school commercial says, 'no, my sister, you gots to get your own!' Anyway, tell us about your recent revelation, Max." Elyce said, clearly trying to change the subject.

"There's really nothing to tell. I barely remembered him from the night we all met but he remembered me. I was in the gym one afternoon—gotta keep this grown body looking young and sexy—and he spotted me. He came over, started to chat bout where we met, helped me with a few exercises and afterwards asked me out for a protein shake."

"What the hell? A shake, not a drink, not dinner? Who does that?" Sienna asked.

"It was all good. He introduced me to something different that I could do each morning to better my health. Besides, we went to dinner later."

"So just when were you going to tell us about you and Max?"

"Honestly, Elyce, I thought you and Sienna would have known by now, being that you're both in some ways involved with his friends."

"Men aren't like us. They don't discuss every single facet of their lives. But hey, it's all good. Where is this heading with you and him?"

"Same place it's heading with you and Xavier, we are just friends. For now!"

"Well alright then." Sienna gave Lana a high five. "That's what's up!"

The ladies finished up their meals and couldn't pass up on the sampler desert platter the pastry chef threw in. It had everything from peach cobbler to coconut cake and everything in between. Everyone ordered their favorite desert to go.

"See you next time, Germany! Tell your parents they did their thing with the food today!"

"Alright, Ms. Xavier. See you soon."

21

"Xavier, I'm just not sure about this trip you've planned. I don't know if I'm ready."

"Really, Elyce? We leave tomorrow, what do you mean you don't think you're ready?"

"Don't you think it's too much too soon?"

Xavier had a smirk on his face and continued to pack his bag. He'd packed cargo shorts, tanks and short sleeve shirts, linen pants, sandals and swimming trunks.

"Look, if you don't want to come, don't come. I'm trying to make an effort here, but I'm not trying to force you to go anywhere with me if you're not comfortable going. Come if you want, stay home if you don't. I've arranged for a car to pick you up at your place and bring you to the airport. You decide what you want to do. If you're not going to come, don't call me to say you're not coming. I'll take the hint and move on. Deal?"

"Wow. Take the hint? What does that mean, Xavier?"

"I'm just saying Elyce, if you think this is too much too soon, ok then. No big deal."

Elyce was silent for several minutes, not knowing what to say or do. She walked over to Xavier who had his back to her as he continued to pack his clothes. She slipped her hands underneath his shirt and began to caress his back with light strokes and squeezes around his shoulders.

"You're way too tense right now. Take your shirt off."

"What?

"Take you shirt off. Cleary, I've upset you. Your whole attitude has changed and not for the better." Elyce pulled him over to the chair in his room, pushed him down and proceeded to take off his shirt.

"Body oil?"

"For what?"

"Do you have it or not?"

"Yes, in the bathroom."

"Great. I'll be right back."

Elyce walked out of the room with the bottle and headed to the kitchen. Xavier heard the door of the microwave open, close, beep, open and close again. When she came back into the room, she had a small bowl of warm oil.

"Now, let's start this conversation again. So, Xavier, what do you think about this trip you've planned for us? Do you think it's too much too soon?" she asked as she began to rub him like a professional masseuse.

"I do not think it's too much too soon. Like I told you before, I'm trying to start over with you as well."

"I see. And where do you think starting over will lead us?"

"Only time will tell. Are you willing to let time tell, doc?"

"We'll see. How does this feel?" she asked as she applies a little pressure to the massage technique she was using.

"Feels great. I guess you were right. I'm super tense right now. I just want things to go well."

"Me too," she whispered in his ear. Elyce walked around and stood in front of Xavier. "You know, I kinda missed you, just a little bit."

"How much is a little bit?"

Elyce held up her thumb and index finger to indicate how much before dropping down to her knees, taking a little more of the oil and beginning to rub it on his chest, lingering a little longer than needed around his nipples. Xavier closed his eyes at her touch and the fact that she was right there in front of him, on her knees. He was trying hard to refrain from making a move. Next thing he felt were her lips on him, causing him to abruptly open his eyes.

"Did I startle you?"

"Absolutely. What are you doing?"

"Didn't you just tell me to loosen up or something? Well, that's what I'm doing."

She leaned in and kissed him again. This time he reciprocated pulling her up to sit on his lap. She decided to straddle him rather than sit in the sideways position he'd put her in. Things were starting to get heated between them. Xavier could feel his dick beginning to fill with blood.

"Um, what are you doing?" he asked as she let her hands travel down towards his pants.

"Nothing," she replied

Elyce began to undo his belt buckle. Feeling the sensation in his pants, Xavier stood up holding her by her thighs, still kissing her. He gently sat her down on the bed, broke away from her lips, dropped to his knees, and slid his hand up the sides of her dress. His touch felt just as amazing as she'd remembered; one that she'd missed but would never admit.

"Lay back," he ordered.

She did as she was told. He gently lifted her hips up, caressing her exposed ass. Disappearing underneath her dress, she felt the sensation of his mouth kissing her through her slightly wet thong. With one hand, he slid the thin piece of fabric to the left and with the other, lifted one leg over his shoulder. Taking his time, he began to lick her outer lips very slowly before finding his way to her clitoris, licking and sucking until it began to swell. His tongue took a deep dive inside her pussy, in and out repeatedly. She was moaning and squirming on the bed.

"You taste better than I remember."

"Ssssshhhhh. This isn't the time for small talk, keep doing what you're doing, please."

Was she pleading with him? Damn right, she hadn't felt the sensation he was giving her for weeks. There's nothing like getting it from a man as opposed to doing it yourself.

Elyce's breathing was rapidly increasing as Xavier kept letting his tongue dance with her body. As she began to cum, he licked faster smashing his tongue to where it covered her clit with the tip inside the warmth of her walls.

"Damn, damn, shit, damn!"

"Come on baby, cum for me, cum for me. I need you to."

"Shit! I'm cumming!"

She released and only heard the lapping sounds of Xavier not missing a single drop. The more he licked, the more she became aroused and within seconds she came again.

"I need to feel you inside me. Please Xavier, let me feel you."

He stood up, looked down at her, kissed her on the forehead.

"That's probably not a good idea. Remember, too much too soon? I don't want to ruin our trip."

"Are you serious?" she asked with a serious tone.

"Yes. Those were your words, remember? I don't want to have sex with you and you have any regrets. If you show up tomorrow, I promise I'll make this trip worth your while. Trust me."

He pulled her dress back down and walked into the bathroom, turned the water on cold as his dick was so erect if felt as if it was going to explode. After a quick ten minutes of relieving himself, he hopped out and called to her from the bathroom.

"Hey, Elyce would you like to order some food?"

There was no answer. He walked out to the bedroom and she wasn't there. He walked out to the living room, not there either. As he passed the foyer, he saw a note taped to the front door.

Thanks, that was marvelous. Sorry! I think I am giving you missed signals with my indecisiveness. I'll let you know when I make it home.

Xavier sat down on his couch with the note in his hand.

"Damn!"

He hoped he hadn't made her run out on their trip. Only time will tell. He grabbed his phone sitting on the coffee table and dialed Nico's number.

"Yo man, it's Xavier. Y'all ready for tomorrow?"

"Dude, you know your number is programmed in my phone right! I know who the hell it is."

"Whatever, Niko. Sienna didn't say anything to Elyce about everyone coming tomorrow, did she?"

"Babe, Xavier wants to know if you or any of the other girls blabbed your big ass mouths to Elyce."

"Say man, stop yelling in my ear already! You weren't supposed to say it like that. You're going to have her cussing me out."

"Tell Xavier's ass ain't nobody said shit to her. He needs to chill the fuck out!"

"You hear that, X?"

"You're such a dick, Niko! I heard her. I'm just hoping Elyce shows up. You know she's still on the fence about it. Ask Sienna to give her a call and try to encourage her to come, ok?"

"You goin' soft man! I ain't never seen you act like this behind a chick."

"Niko, she's just not any chick. Hell, you know it's gotta to be something about her to make me turn down all the pussy I've been used to getting. She could be the one, for real.

"Shut the fuck up, man. You serious?"

"Dead ass! Make sure Sienna makes that call, man. I'll holla at you tomorrow and hopefully I won't be the solo dude in the group."

"I got you, X. Peace."

Elyce stood in her shower enjoying the stream of hot water splashing against her body; her mind racing back and forth to the last two hours. A smile crept across her face. Just as she stepped out,

Sienna was calling her up via video chat. She grabbed her robe and accepted the call still dripping wet.

"What's up, E! Damn girl, you just get out the shower? You're looking like a wet poodle."

"Hi to you too, Sienna. What's up?"

"Nothing much. Just checking on you."

"Thanks, girl. I'm trying to clear my head and figure out what I'm going to do about this trip with Xavier tomorrow."

"Really, E? What's to figure out? You know you want to go, so quit pretending."

"I do want to go and after tonight, I am strongly considering it."

"After tonight? What the hell are you talking about girl?"

"Nothing. I had a chat with Xavier and I think his actions were enough to change my mind."

"A chat, huh. You sure that's all you did was chat?"

"Girl, yes!" Elyce relayed strongly, knowing it was a lie.

"Yeah, ok. Whatever. But in my opinion, and it's just my opinion, take it for what it's worth. It's a trip to Anguilla with water and beach and Caribbean life. You know how much you love the beach. You should go. Even if nothing comes of it, and you and Xavier decide to go your separate ways, you would have taken that trip and had some fun."

"It's not like I can't take myself, Sienna."

"I didn't say you couldn't. How often do you have a guy who's willing to take you somewhere? If I recall, you invited that punk ass Lance with you to visit your folks; he didn't invite you anywhere."

“Don’t remind me, girl! I’ll sleep on it and see how I feel in the morning.”

“You do that! I’ll talk to you later.”

“Later, chick. Thanks for checking on me!”

“Of course!”

22

The knock on the door startled Elyce, she wasn't expecting anyone.

"Who is it?"

"Car service, ma'am; here for your pick up."

Elyce opened the door.

"Sorry. I forgot you were coming. Can you give me 10 minutes to finish throwing a few things in my bag and I'll be right out?"

"Sure, ma'am. No problem."

"And don't call Xavier either. You got it!"

"Yes, ma'am. He'd given us a directive not call him anyway."

"Oh. Ok. Be right out."

"Yes, ma'am." he replied.

Elyce closed the door and went back to grab her suitcase. Good thing it had roller wheels because she'd packed way more than she could ever need. She had multiple bathing suits, shorts, sundresses, sandals, etc. For the trip itself, she decided to wear a beautiful fuchsia one shoulder halter dress that was fitted at the top, lose and flowing at the bottom with a thigh high split accompanied by a pair of jeweled sandals. Since she loved the beach, she decided to wash her hair and pull her spiral curls back into a ponytail with a matching her hair band. When she opened the door, the driver was still standing there.

"Ready, miss?"

"Sure am. Let's get this show on the road."

While in the back of the SUV, Elyce figured she should text her girls and let them know what she decided to do.

Hey heifa's ~ I know you all are wondering what I was going to do regarding my trip to Anguilla with Xavier. In the car headed to the airport now!

Seemed like she'd just hit send and she received a response from Jayce.

Great bitch! Glad you're going. Lawd knows you've had a stick up your ass forever. Keep an open mind, relax and have fun. Elyce couldn't help but laugh.

"Of course, she would say that."

"Excuse me, ma'am. What did you say?"

"Oh nothing, just talking to myself. What's your name by the way?"

"It's Robert, ma'am."

"Nice to meet you, Robert."

"Same here, ma'am."

"Please call me Elyce. My mother is ma'am."

"Yes, ma'am—I mean, Elyce. Will do."

As they were riding along, Elyce noticed they'd passed the exit for the airport.

"Robert, you missed the exit for the airport. Are you going to turn around soon?"

"No, ma'am. We are not going to the commercial terminal; we are going to the private terminal."

"Private? What the fuck? Sorry, Robert. I didn't mean to say that last part out loud."

"It's ok, ma'am. It's not my job to judge, but to drive you safely to your destination." Elyce smiled and immediately began to text again.

Ok, ok, Xavier has lost his mind. We are taking a private plane for this trip! Can you believe it? He really is trying to make this trip great. I think he's off to a good start.

Once again, her phone beeped immediately. This time it was Sienna.

Well sit back, relax, and enjoy the ride. Now stop texting us and get your head in the game! Have fun. Elyce smiled again.

"Whew!" Sienna exhaled. "I'm glad that girl is just texting instead of calling. I think the surprise would get totally blown if she called," she whispered to Jayce and Lana.

"Yeah, you're so right, Sienna. She is going to be so surprised when she sees all of us on this plane, too." Jayce added. The ladies were whispering, not wanting Xavier to hear their conversation.

"Xavier, you're a good man! You did this."

"Thanks, Jayce. I'm just hopeful that your girl shows up. We will wait 20 more minutes; the driver knows that's my cutoff. If she doesn't come, I'm going to take my stuff off the plane and you guys go ahead and have a great time." There was a little sadness in his voice when he said that last sentence.

"She may be stubborn most of the time but she ain't stupid."

"I sure hope you're right about that, Lana. I'm going to go stand outside. Y'all lower the shades, I don't want her to suspect a thing until she steps inside the plane."

"Aww, he looks like he's filled with uncertainty about whether or not her ass will show up. Should I tell him?" Jayce asked.

"Babe, no. You should not tell him. We'll be her surprise and she'll be his. This is going to be a great trip," Tariq replied

"You're right, babe. Can't wait until she gets here."

No sooner than Jayce finished her sentence, they heard a car door close. Elyce had arrived.

"You look beautiful today. I was beginning to think you weren't going to come," Xavier said as he extended his hand to walk her to the plane.

"Thanks, Xavier," she said with a smirk. "I know Robert told you I was coming."

"No, he didn't actually. I gave him very explicit instructions not to contact me whether you were or were not in the car."

"Oh, I see. So, a private plane? What's up with this?"

They walked over to the bottom of the stairs where a gentleman was standing in a pilot's uniform.

"Elyce, this is Captain Anthony. Owner of this beautiful Gulfstream aptly called *The Dreamer*. He is also a long-term client of mine."

"Nice to meet you, Elyce. Xavier speaks very highly of you. I'm happy to be your captain today."

"Nice to meet you as well, Captain Anthony. I'm looking forward to a wonderful flight."

"Alrighty, let's get you onboard Elyce. Robert will load your luggage."

"Ok, Xavier. Thanks for the ride, Robert."

"No problem, ma'am."

Xavier pulled out a diva sleep mask and handed to Elyce.

"I need you to put this on. I have a surprise for you."

"Isn't flying a private jet enough of a surprise?"

"Well, I guess that can be taken into consideration but, I think this one will be up there as well. So, put it on please and let's go."

"Wait, how am I supposed to see where I'm going?"

"You'll have to listen as I talk or I can carry you. What's your preference?"

"Geez, Xavier. I'll just listen."

Xavier stood behind Elyce with his hands on her hips as he guided her up the short flight of stairs making sure to tell her when to step up. Once they got just inside the door of the plane, he told her to stop. Let go of her and stood behind her.

"Are you ready for your surprise?"

"Sure, I guess. I'm not sure what more you can do today."

"Ok, take off your mask."

"Surprise!" everyone on the plane yelled. Her whole crew and their men were sitting on board.

"Oh, hell naw! You all were in on this! What if I hadn't come? I can't believe you, Xavier." She turned around and punched him jokingly in the shoulder.

Xavier stood there with a wide grin on his face.

"Bitch, if you hadn't come, you'd be sitting your ass in town all by your lonesome because we were going with or without you!"

"Shut up, Jayce! Y'all wouldn't have gone without me!"

"The hell you say," Lana added. "How often do you get a free trip with good friends and family on a private damn jet? Shit. It would have been bye, bye Elyce. 'Wish you were here' on a postcard."

"Wow, Xavier. You're just full of surprises. Anything else?"

"Naw, I don't think so. Just the look of surprise and the smile on your face right now is enough for one day! Have a seat. Cesilie, our flight attendant and Captain's wife, will get us some drinks for the flight. Thanks, everyone, for clearing your schedules and, more importantly, not letting her in on the surprise."

"Naw, man, thank you for this trip!" Niko gave Xavier a thumbs up as he leaned over to kiss Sienna.

"No problem. Y'all my dudes, your ladies are her girls, and Tariq, you're family so it's all good. Captain, I do believe we are ready to go!"

After flying over the beautiful island water and beach, it seemed as if they would never get through customs with the extra-long lines.

"Dang, Lana. How heavy is your bag? You must have brought everything except the kitchen sink."

"Shut up, Elyce! I couldn't decide on what to wear. Hell, we are going to be here an entire week. I needed at least three outfits a day." Max shook his head since he was the one pulling the stuffed bag.

"Who in the hell changes their clothes three times a day on vacation? You're on the beach most of the day so a swimsuit and an evening outfit should have been enough."

"OK, Jayce and Elyce, y'all lay off my girl. She has to be ready for her man."

"You got that right, baby! See, y'all, Max has my back."

Everyone began to laugh because Max was behind Lana mouthing he'd told her not to pack so much stuff.

"What you say, Max?"

"I said you're going to get your world rocked in every one of those outfits. The neighbors will know my name."

"Boy, you a fool!"

"A man has to do what a man has to do to keep his woman happy, Xavier. Sorta like this elaborate trip you've planned."

"Dayum!" Tariq said with his hand over his mouth. "Max got you, bruh."

"Ain't no biggie. Elyce is well worth this and more. I'm going to do what I need to do to get her back on a permanent basis. But y'all wouldn't know anything about that. Right, Tariq?"

"Man, I just appreciate the invitation. So, whatever you say, bruh. I totally agree." Xavier just shook his head and chuckled at Tariq's comeback.

After everyone made it through customs, the group headed out towards ground transportation where the villa they'd be staying in sent four luxury SUVs to pick them up.

"Lana, if your luggage doesn't fit in one car, I'm sure there's room in the others."

"Oh, not you too, Xavier! Whatever. I don't care what y'all trash talking about over there. Don't be mad at me when I'm fly all day, every day."

"Hush, lady! Get in the car so we can get this trip started," Max said as he moved Lana towards the awaiting open door of the all white on white vehicle.

Inside the car, each couple had a welcome message, chocolate covered strawberries, and various premium alcohols with mixers.

"Welcome to the island, Mr. Tuft and Ms. Xavier. My name is Lee and I will be your designated driver during your stay here with us. Of course, the villa has a rental car company on property if you decide you'd like to explore the island on your own time. We offer plenty of beach activities like parasailing, water skis and paddle boats. And there is a ferry that leaves several times a day that drops off at neighboring islands or you can catch a sea plane as well. Whatever you desire during your stay, we'll do our very best to make it happen for you."

"Wow! Thanks, Lee. It sounds like you can't do anything but have a great time with all of those amenities available," Elyce replied.

"Yes, ma'am."

"And Xavier, if I haven't said this already, thank you for arranging this trip and inviting my friends along. I don't even want to think about what this is costing you."

"Sssshhhh," Xavier said as he placed a finger over Elyce's lips. "Cost is not a factor to be concerned with on this trip. All that matters is that you have a good time."

Elyce couldn't help but open her mouth and suck on Xavier's index finger that was lingering on her lips. His eyes widened at her gesture as the blood was beginning to course through his body heading straight to his penis. He pulled his finger out of her mouth and quickly grabbed something cold to drink.

"You know what that does to me. Don't start anything you're not going to finish lady." Elyce shrugged her shoulders, cracked a wicked half smile, and relaxed back in her seat.

"OK, Mr. Tuft. Have it your way."

Her body was on fire inside and her abrupt actions left her with moisture she could feel on her inner thighs as she crossed and uncrossed her legs. The cars pulled up in unison in the driveway of the home away from home over the next week. It was adorned with an array of beautiful flowers in bright colors surrounding a waterfall that seemed to dance to the acoustic jazz coming through the speakers. As the group exited the vehicles, they were greeted by bellmen who swiftly collected their luggage and handed them the keys to their villas.

Once inside the grand lobby area with its soft white marble floors, elaborate columns, and buttery leather furniture, hostesses met the group with warm hellos and offered them the beverage of the day; a delicious pear infused drink with or without the vodka. Elyce quickly grabbed a glass with vodka hoping it would help in calming her fire down below.

"Ladies and gentlemen, welcome! My name is Remi, your concierge. If there is anything that you need during your stay, just call me or one of the other staff persons on duty for assistance. Your rooms are all set, just follow your luggage and we do hope you enjoy your stay."

"Thank you," everyone seemed to say in unison, following their luggage as they were told.

"This villa is absolutely amazing, Xavier! It's like a mini mansion."

Elyce walked from one room to the next finally settling on the bedroom upstairs where the bathroom had a large two-person tub with built in seat backs so couples could face each other and see out the big bay windows overlooking the pale blue ocean waters. The more she explored, the moister she became. Xavier remained downstairs waiting for the bellman to return so he could give him a proper tip before heading upstairs to join Elyce. She was standing on the balcony of the bedroom, waving frantically as he walked up behind her. All the couples were on their balconies in utter awe of their villas as well as the property itself.

“Bro! For real man, thanks,” Niko shouted which was followed by more “thank you”s.

“No problem, y’all. I’m glad you like your space. Let’s meet in the lobby at six for dinner and to figure out our plans for tomorrow. Deuces!”

Xavier grabbed Elyce by the hand, pulled her away from the balcony and closed the doors as the palm trees swayed back and forth from the island breeze. He sat down on the edge of the chaise lounge and watched Elyce as she stood there watching the trees. And suddenly without warning, the straps of her sundress slid off her shoulders. She turned around and began to walk towards him stepping out of her shoes along the way. Her excitement below hadn’t subsided at all and her pussy began to throb in anticipation of once again feeling Xavier inside of her.

“Sit back,” she commanded as her dress fell to the floor exposing her breast and erect nipples. He spotted the wetness of her panties and smiled.

“What are you doing, doc?”

“Finishing what I started.”

She grabbed his hand and again sucked his index finger before removing it from the warmth of her mouth. She trailed his hand pass her collarbone, over her erect nipple, down past her belly button, turning it palm side up, and into the wetness of her panties. Xavier couldn’t believe how wet she was or that she was being very direct about what she wanted. She straddled him, his hand still inside her panties, gently moving back and forth with an occasional touch of her clitoris which at this point was enlarged itself. Unbuttoning, unzipping, and pulling his penis from his pants in record time, she moved his hand, untied the side strings holding her panties and slid him inside.

"Wait, wait. Don't you want me to get a condom," he whispered.

"You been fucking other people?"

"No!" he moaned already feeling the wetness of her on him.

"Do you have a disease?"

"Hell no!" he laughed. "Always get my regular check ups."

"Well, stop talking and fuck me!"

Xavier's eyes widened as he looked up at this beautiful woman whose hips were rocking back and forth while her vaginal walls squeezed and released around him.

"Whatever you wish, it's my duty to oblige, beautiful."

Xavier continued to let Elyce ride his dick to satisfaction. He removed the band holding her hair and let it fall down her back and shoulders running his fingers through it. He cupped the back of her neck and pulled her mouth towards his kissing her passionately. She moaned loudly as she released, her cream seeping all over the pants he was wearing. Her hips continued moving in the motion of a figure eight and Xavier soon released all he had inside of her. Collapsing on him, they laid there in silence not speaking a word, just listening to the breaths they were both taking. A movie line came to Xavier's mind during their silence.

"'It's not how many breaths you take but the moments that take your breath away.' You are one of those moments for me, Elyce."

23

The table was covered with beautiful tiger lilies neatly placed above each of the dinner plates. Ocean waves lit only by the moon provided a nice soundtrack for relaxation. As the group approached the table, they were greeted by the sounds of steel drums beating and Remi. Elyce had changed into a lavender, off-the-shoulder sundress, which looked amazing against her bronze skin and curly sandy hair. Her eyes were a piercing gray that she'd kept hidden behind her transition lenses earlier in the day.

"There's Remi, Xavier. My goodness, she is stunning. Don't you think?"

"Sure, Elyce. But I'm not concerned with her beauty, only yours today and everyday."

"Good evening, ladies and gentlemen. I trust you've settled into your rooms okay."

"Yes, Remi. Everything is absolutely perfect. Thank you for everything you've done to make my friends comfortable," Xavier responded.

"You're welcome, Mr. Tuft."

“Xavier. Please call me Xavier. Mr. Tuft is my dad, except when I’m at work.”

“Okay, okay. I’ve got you. We’ve arranged for an evening of entertainment and we hope your friends aren’t shy. We’ll be looking for dancers.”

“Oh, we’re all over that. I, for one, am a great dancer,” Jayce interjected.

“Um Jayce, you’re on your own with that one,” Tariq responded.

“Tariq, babe, we are on vacation. We are going to have fun.” Jayce winked at him and rubbed his thigh.

“Don’t we always have fun? We don’t need public dancing for that. Remember St. Croix?” Jayce couldn’t help but grin from ear to ear thinking back on the time they had during that trip, but her thoughts were quickly interrupted.

“Thank you for volunteering, Miss Jayce. I’ll make sure the dancers know where you’re sitting. Now, please have a seat everyone as your food is approaching,” Remi instructed.

The men pulled out the chairs for the women and the servers approached the table carrying multiple bowls of divine smelling food.

“Is that callaloo and curried goat, Remi?”

“Yes, Miss Sienna. What do you know about callaloo?”

“Me got some island roots there, gurl.”

“You don’t say now? Where’ bouts you from?” Remi asked.

“Well, I’m from the states but my grandmother was born and raised in St. Maarten. I used to come down here and spend my summers as a young girl. In fact, we need to take a trip over there for a visit, you guys.”

“Sounds good to me, babe. What y’all think?” Niko asked.

“We’re on vacation,” Lana added. “We don’t have anything set in stone so let’s just put that on a list of things to do while we’re here.”

“Sounds like the beginnings of fun things ahead on this trip. But I’m starving and ready to eat this food that is calling my name or maybe that’s my stomach saying, ‘Jayce, feed me right damn now!’”

Everyone laughed at Jayce’s comment but didn’t hesitate to hurriedly fix their plates full of goat, jerk chicken, blue marlin, plantains, rice and peas, callaloo, cassava, and more. Suddenly, there was a quick tap on the glass by Max.

“Before we get our grub on, we need to bless this food. Xavier, go ahead man.”

“You go ahead and knock that out since it’s your recommendation, Max.”

“Fine. Heavenly father, we are humbly here before you through your traveling grace and mercies. We thank you for this food we are about to receive for the nourishment of our bodies, which also nourishes our minds and souls. Bless the preparers and the consumers. In your righteous and holy name, we all pray, Amen.”

“Amen,” the group said in unison.

There was very little chatter but lots of forks clinging during dinner. Just as everyone finished up their desserts, as if on cue, a group of men came over to the table and pulled Jayce up out of her seat and instinctively, she grabbed Lana and pulled her up too.

“Alright Miss Jayce, we hear you wanted to dance, so now it’s time,” the gentlemen said in his island accent. Jayce suddenly wanted to back out of that big talk she’d spoke of earlier and as Lana tried to leave, Jayce pulled her back pleading with her friend.

"Come on, girl, don't leave me out here by myself."

"You're the one saying you had it, Jayce. I'm going to sit down and watch you do your thing, missy," Lana replied.

"No, no, no. Please, girl. Stay out here with me." Lana broke away from Jayce and went back to her seat next to Max.

"Why you leave her out there alone, Lana?"

"Max, I am not about to make a fool of myself in front of you just yet."

"You do remember that I was at the birthday party, right?"

"Did you just bring up that awful party, Max? Really?" Lana said sadly.

"I'm just saying. I've seen you make a fool of yourself, so this dancing isn't a big deal. Come on, Lana, loosen up a little bit and go up there with your future daughter-in-law." Lana gave Max that mean mug look. She rolled her eyes and folded her arms.

"Oh, so you're not going to go up there and shake a little something for me, baby? Come on, I need to know if you can move something or if you're all uptight?"

"Well, Max, if you want to see if I can move, we need to leave this table right now."

"Excuse y'all!" Sienna interrupted, "Hold all that nasty talk till later."

"Mind your business, babe!"

"Whatever, Niko. Ain't nobody in nobody else's business."

"Sounds like you're all up in it. Why don't you focus on getting some of your own with me?" Niko placed his hand on Sienna back and smiled.

"Thanks, Niko. Get your woman, please!" Lana said with a laugh.

"The hell with you, Lana. Why don't you take your butt back up there with Jayce? Looks like she needs some help," Sienna said with a tone.

"Maybe you should go then and get out my damn conversation with my man," Lana replied with the same tone.

Things were beginning to sound a little too intense for Elyce as she was trying not to get in the middle if they were just joking around.

"Ladies, ladies, come on, let's not have friction our first night. I'm going out here with Jayce. Y'all comin'?"

"Yeah, E," Sienna replied. "I'm coming before Lana and I ruin the night. I was just joking but you know how she gets."

Xavier smacked Elyce on the butt when she got up to head towards the dance area.

"Ouch! Man, you know you're going to have to rub that later." Elyce rubbed her butt as she headed towards the floor.

"Don't worry, I have every intention of doing just that! Now get out there, save your girl, and show me what you got."

Lana grabbed Max's hand pulling him to his feet.

"Let's go. I need to take a walk and calm down. I don't even know what that was all about in the first place. I'm trippin."

"Say man, do you see our ladies up there shakin' and poppin' like professionals?" Niko asked Xavier.

"Yeah, I see them."

Bruh, if Sienna, Jayce and Elyce can pop it like that, I have some questions for them. Sienna hasn't shown me anything like that ever," Niko said with wide eyes.

"Well, all of them have the bodies to make that booty jiggle like that. I ain't mad at them," Xavier added.

"I ain't mad either X; I definitely ain't mad. But I will be looking for a private show a little later on. Tariq, what you know about that?" Niko said jokingly.

"I'm not one to kiss and tell man, so I'll let you two brothers get your answers from your ladies."

The fellas gave each other a fist bump, picked up their glasses and clinked them together.

"What was that all about?" Elyce asked as she found her way back over to Xavier.

"What was all that out there about from the three of you?" Xavier asked with a sly grin.

"What are you talking about? Sienna, Jayce and I were just out there dancing. You did tell me to go out there and help my girl out."

"I think you ladies were doing a lot more than just dancing. Sienna, is there something you want to tell me?" Niko questioned.

"No, baby. There's absolutely nothing I want to tell you. When the girls get together on the dance floor, we just let loose as the music takes us away."

"Let loose, huh?"

"Yes, Niko. Let loose."

"I'll need you to let loose, pop it and drop it when we get back to the room tonight then, since you can let loose so well."

"Yeah, me too!" Xavier added.

"You too what, Xavier?"

"What Niko said! I want to see that later, too. My own little private show." The ladies all looked at each other and just bust out laughing and sat down with their guys.

"Hey, where did Lana go?" Sienna asked the guys.

"She left after you and her had those minor words."

"Seriously, Niko? She left?"

"What minor words?" Jayce asked.

"Her and Max were talking a little nasty, I jokingly told them to hold it down and she got all defensive talking about I was all up in her business. Chile, please. It's just Lana and her foolishness. Ain't nobody got time for that."

"Tariq, baby, you want to go look for them?"

"No. She's a grown woman. I'm on vacation, having a good time and her antics have caused me enough drama to last me a lifetime. This, right here, is our time and all I want to do is spend these days in paradise lovin' on you." Tariq wrapped Jayce in his big strong arms and kissed her lovingly. It seemed like the kiss of a lifetime as it kept going on and on.

"Get a room!" Xavier said through a cough. They broke away from each other and Jayce's grin seemed wider than the full moon hovering above their heads. She gave the girls a quick wink and began to fan herself.

"Babe, we've given these bustas enough of a peep show," Tariq said.

"Damn sho did," Sienna added.

"Whatever, girl! We are going to part company with you good people and go enjoy that gorgeous sunken tub in our room and some. You may want to close your balcony doors in case Tariq gets too loud."

Tariq had a blank look on his face at Jayce's statement but didn't say a word. He didn't want to interrupt the way his lady was feeling right now because it was about to go down.

"Goodnight y'all." Tariq & Jayce linked arms together and walked back to their room while the two remaining couples listened to music, danced and had a few more drinks before saying goodnight as well. As they walked along the lit pathway back to the villas, it was so quiet. All you could hear were the chirps from the crickets and the other critters out in the night air.

"Xavier, let's go sit in that hammock over there for a little while."

"Whatever you like, miss lady."

"Goodnight, Niko & Sienna; we'll see you in the morning for our beach horseback ride."

"Cool," Niko responded. "Goodnight to you, too."

The hammocks were spacious enough for four people to fit in and were even covered with a sheer net to keep the night flyers away. Elyce removed her shoes and Xavier lifted her up and laid her on the swing.

"You good, beautiful? Do you need anything to drink before I get in?"

"No, Xavier. I'm good. Come on in here and lay with me please."

Xavier walked around to the other side and climbed inside with her. She turned on her side and positioned herself so they were spooning.

"Mmmmmm! This is nice, Ms. Xavier."

"Yes, Mr. Tuft, it most certainly is. I just want to lay here, comfortably in your arms and just listen to the sounds of our breaths."

"OK."

24

"Babe, come out here for a minute," Jayce called to Tariq.

She was standing out on the balcony of their villa bedroom. It was really dark except for the moonlight and the dim light emanating from their room. Tariq came out with a towel wrapped around his waist, body still glistening from the oils they'd used during their baths.

"It's beautiful out here. Just like you, J. I love you very much and don't ever want to be without you."

"I don't want to be without you either, Tariq."

She pulled him closer to her and began to place soft kisses on his chest, stomach and neck. She walked behind him and continued to trail soft kisses across his back. His body would flinch just a little with each peck she placed. Reaching around, she placed her hand between the slit in his towel and slowly began to stroke his dick as he stood there with his legs slightly parted.

"Turn around," she whispered. "Stay right here for just one moment."

Jayce disappeared back into the room then out of sight. When she reappeared, she was carrying a duvet cover, a sheet and three pillows. She spread the comforter out laying right between the balcony doors and the railing stopping right where Tariq was standing. She dropped two pillows at the top and one at his feet. Kissing him deeply, thrusting her tongue around in his mouth, she licked his lips and resumed planting soft kisses on his cheek, his neck, his nipples, his stomach, his hips, bending herself over then dropping to her knees. Without warning, she slipped his erect dick into her mouth causing his knees to buckle from the anticipation. He began to move his pelvis in and out of her mouth as the blood continued to make its way to the engorged veins in his penis.

"Shit baby, that feels so good."

She continued to suck harder, cupping his balls in her hands and taking swaps at them with her tongue as his dick danced in the back of her throat. His body was tense and shaking. She grabbed his ass checks and began to squeeze them as she thrust him harder and harder into her warm mouth.

"Aaaaahhhhhh, shit. I'm coming baby, I'm coming so hard rrrrrriiiiiiiggggghhhhhhtttttt now!" he yelled as he released cum all inside of her mouth.

Jayce didn't move; she kept him inside her mouth as his salty release eased its way across her palate and down her throat. It was so much, some of it began to seep out the corners of her mouth landing on her breast. She took his hands and placed them on her chest moving them in a circular motion until her nipples harden themselves. Releasing his dick from the clasp of her jaws, he dropped down to his knees, looked her in the eyes.

"You keep doing that shit to me, I'll be looking for you in the daytime with a flashlight." She laughed so hard at him and gave him a huge hug.

“One second, baby. I’ll be right back.”

Tariq swatted at her ass as she ran off, again.

“You’ve got to be fucking kidding me. Did you see that shit, Xavier?”

“Yes, E. I saw it. That Jayce is a beast with the fellatio. Do friends of a feather flock together?”

“Ha, ha. I don’t know about all of that. But maybe you’ll find out.”

“It’s not a big deal to me, at least not at this moment. All that matters right now is me being here with you, Elyce.”

“Is that right? Just how much does it not matter?”

“Would you like me to tell you or show you?”

“Be creative. I think you can do both.”

Xavier’s eye’s widened at her statement but always up to a challenge, he decided to let his lips and hands do the talking. Covering her lips with his, he kissed her while using his free hand to roll her on her back. The cool breeze from the swing rocking back and forth had her hair blowing back and forth in her face. He gently lifted her head and placed her hair behind it and resumed kissing her.

Xavier allowed his hand to caress the side of her face, her neck and travel to the top of her sundress where he let it rest briefly before fondling her nipple as it poked through the cotton material. Elyce began to move slightly, breaking away from their kiss. Xavier didn’t let that stop him but instead took the opportunity to pull her dress down just above her rib cage leaving her breast exposed to the night air. He immediately covered one with his hand, the other with his mouth while his free hand traveled down to her legs.

“Open,” he whispered.

She obliged as his hand rubbed her outer left thigh and her inner right, down one, up the other. He continued this dance with his fingertips for what seemed like an eternity but was only seconds in actuality. His hand began to travel north towards her pussy and to his surprise, she wasn't wearing any panties any longer. She'd snuck and taken them off somewhere between them going to dinner and coming back to the hammock. That definitely made it easier for him.

He raised his hand to her mouth and inserted his finger. She sucked it as if it were his penis. Once it was nice and wet, he removed it from her mouth and slowly inserted it inside of her.

"How am I doing so far?" he asked while slowly moving his finger it in and out of her pussy to match the circulation motion of her hips adding an additional two fingers inside her. Her breathing became shallow, as there was a slight arch beginning to form in her back.

"Oh, Xavier. You're doing great," she said far above a whisper.

"Shhh. You don't want anybody to hear us, do you?"

"I don't give a fuck right now."

"Oh, you don't? Ok then."

With what he deemed was permission to drive her crazy, he flicked her clit with his tongue.

"Oh yes. Suck it, baby."

Those words seemed to turn Xavier on even more. With is fingers still inside her, he maneuvered himself out of the hammock and turned her body sideways ever so gently. He pushed her left leg up then her right, so he could have complete access to her wet pussy that was hidden by the length of her dress. Glancing up to see her face, her eyes were closed, her bottom lip clinched between her teeth and her hands on her breast, pinching her nipples between her thumb and forefinger.

"You ready?" he asked.

"Yes, yes. I'm ready for whatever you have to give me, mister."

Bending at the waist, Xavier disappeared from sight underneath her sundress where he took his time sucking on her clit, licking her outer and inner lips between deep dips inside her pussy. Fast and slow, he toyed with her while nothing but his face touched her as he used his hands to steady the hammock. He took the tip of his tongue and swirled it in a circular fashion over her clit, her lips and her open hole. Without losing contact with her skin, he moved his head up and down ever so slowly. Without warning, he used his lips to roll his tongue and stick it as deep inside her has it would go while licking her juices over her clit until she came.

"Damn, Xavier! What the hell was that you put inside me?" He smiled, showing her all 32 of his beautiful teeth before partially closing his mouth showing her how he rolls his tongue.

"Well, damn. That shit was fucking amazing. I came so hard I don't think I can feel my legs right now."

Xavier laughed. He slipped his shoes back on, bent over and picked hers up, handing them to her.

"What do you want me to do with these?"

"Do your hands work, lady?"

"You see that they do."

"Okay then. You hold your shoes and I'm going to carry you back to our room. I'm not done with you yet!"

"Alright then. I like the way that sounds." Elyce smiled.

"Oh yeah? Well, tell me how this sounds. I'm glad you came on this trip. I need you to know that I care about you and I'm trying to show you that you are my priority." Elyce gave Xavier her best pouty mouth look.

"I don't really want to have that discussion tonight. Let's just keep what we started in that hammock going and talk about priorities later. Okay?"

"Sure. No problem." Xavier felt a little defeated but was hopeful that a night of good fucking would help to change her mind.

"Oh my gosh! Who the hell is calling the room this early in the damn morning? Hello," Elyce answered with an irritated tone.

"Hey, sunshine!"

"Really, Sienna. Why are you calling so early?"

"Heifa, it's 10:15. It ain't damn early."

"What? It's 10:15 already? Don't we have reservations to ride at 11:15?"

"Yes, we do. That's why I'm calling you. Everyone is having breakfast now and making plans for St. Maarten later."

"Everybody?"

"Yes."

"Lana too?"

"Yes, even her crazy ass. I swear she needs some medication or something. Poor Max. I hope he knows what he's in for."

"Girl, me too. OK, let me get Xavier up and we'll be down there shortly. Can you fix us a plate of fruit, some grits, turkey sausage and juice, please? I'm sure they'll be closed before we get down there."

"Sure, nasty girl. Just bring your ass on down here. Don't be having morning shower sex."

"What? What are you talking about?"

"Niko and I saw y'all in that hammock last night. Shit got me so hot, I fucked the shit out of him all over that villa."

"Oh, hell. What Niko say?"

"He was like, 'that's my boy. All up in that pussy.'"

"How did y'all see us? We thought you went up to your room."

"We did but I left my hat, so we took a stroll to go get it and on the way back, we saw y'all. Well, we saw you but only saw Xavier from the shoulders down cuz he was face deep in pussy. But thank you, girl! Now get your ass down here."

"I'm so embarrassed. Okay, be there shortly."

Elyce hung up the phone and kissed Xavier on his back. He stirred a little but didn't wake up.

"Hey, sleepy head. Time to get up."

"What time is it?"

"It's 10:20, Xavier. We have to get up, get dressed and get ready to leave. We're riding at 11:15."

"Okay, okay. I'm trying to move but I'm sticking to the sheets."

"Must be all that cum I squeezed out of you last night," Elyce laughed, got out of the bed and headed towards the bathroom. "Come on, get up. And by the way, your boy Niko saw you face deep in pussy last night."

"Shit! I can only imagine what kind of shit he'll be talking today then."

"Hey, I don't care what he or Sienna say. I so enjoyed you last night. Can't wait to do it again tomorrow."

"Tomorrow? What's wrong with tonight?"

"My girl is a little sore after last night. I don't know if she'll be ready, but we'll see."

Xavier stood up out the bed and his dick was erect again. He walked towards Elyce who was bent over at the sink brushing her teeth. He stuck his dick between her legs.

"We got time for a quickie?"

"Didn't I just tell you she's sore? Get your horny ass in the shower and calm that thing down."

"Fine then."

When they reached the group, everyone was sitting back rubbing their stomachs talking about how full they were from that delicious breakfast.

"So happy you all could join us. Musta been some night," Max said.

"I'm sure mine and Xavier's night was no different from anyone else's. So, let's just leave it at that and keep this beautiful day going. Sienna, you hook a sista up with some food?"

"Yes, girl. Here you go."

"Thanks. Here's a little something to hold us over until lunch, Xavier. I'm sure we don't want to ride on an empty stomach."

"I'm sure this ride won't be as much fun as the one last night," Xavier whispered in her ear.

Elyce squeezed Xavier at the knee and gave him that "don't talk no shit in front of them" look. He smiled, squeezed her hand and gave her a wink and quickly changed the conversation to the group.

"So, is everyone having a good time so far?" he asked.

"We're only a few days in. I'm looking forward to some non-group activity stuff," Lana responded.

"Why is that, Lana?" Xavier inquired.

"Just want to take some time and do some things, just me and Max you know."

"Well, I'm sure the group wouldn't object to you doing that so y'all do your thing," he responded with shrug. Max looked around the table at his friends.

"Don't I get a say? Am I not part of this equation and decision making?" he asked.

"What? Don't you want to spend some alone time, just me and you, Max?" Lana asked sounding a bit defensive.

"It's not like we don't spend time together at night. Why do you want to go off from the group? I'm not with that right now," Max replied sternly.

"Well, fine. Fuck it then. You hang with them for as long as you like, and I'll find something else to do on my own." Lana folded her arms and rolled her eyes like a two-year-old.

"Now you're trippin'. Please don't start this day off with your attitude. Do you see anybody else acting like you are?" Max asked, waving his hands towards the friends.

Lana looked around at everyone at the table who were all staring at her.

“Shit. I’m tripping, huh?” she said softly.

“Hell yeah, your ass is trippin’. Again! This is paradise. Act like it, bitch,” Jayce chimed in. “We’re trying to be sensitive to you, but you don’t give a damn.”

“Why I gotta be a bitch, Jayce?”

“Cuz that’s how you’ve been acting ever since you found out about Tariq and me. Well, we and everyone else, I’m sure, is here on this gorgeous island to have a good time and enjoy the good company of each other. If you’re going to ruin it for the rest of us, I’ll personally buy your ass a plane ticket and you can go the fuck home. Get a fuckin’ grip!”

Jayce got up from the table and walked off towards the beach. Tariq followed behind her until he caught up, grabbed her hand and pulled her close to him.

“Hey, hey. I know you’re tired of her bullshit and so am I, but this is not the time. Let’s ignore that and focus on us and having the time our of lives.” She smiled weakly at Tariq. He had so much compassion.

“I love your little young ass, man!”

“Oh, you talking shit about my being young huh? I didn’t hear any complaints from you last night.”

“Your ability to fuck and being a youngster don’t have anything to do with the other. But know this: I really do love you Tariq and I look forward to the day I become your wife.”

“Well, we’re here, ain’t nothing to it but to do it.”

“Lana would fucking flip out for real. Plus, my parents would flip out on me, too. You know they probably thought I’d be an old maid,” Jayce laughed and hugged Tariq tightly. “If you still want to marry me after this trip, we can go to the courthouse when we get back to the states."

"Trust me lady, nothing is going to make me change my mind about making this 'til death do us part."

"Alright, alright, break all that lovey dovey stuff up! Let's get our ride on," Xavier said as he walked past the two lovebirds. "He's wide open for her, Elyce. That's a beautiful thing. Don't you agree?"

"Sure. Whatever you say." Xavier snatched Elyce up off the ground and spun her around a few times. "Put me down, man. You're acting like a big silly kid."

"Hey, life can't always be full of seriousness. If it were," Xavier got close to her ear, so she could hear his whisper, "your pussy wouldn't be so sore!" He put her down, slapped her on the ass and ran off.

"Punk!" she yelled at him.

25

"That ride was amazing you guys," Elyce squealed. "Didn't y'all enjoy that? Xavier, did you enjoy it?"

"I think everyone had a good time," Xavier responded.

"Well, I had more than a good time," Elyce stated. "I mean sitting on top of that stallion as it trotted through the sand right into the ocean was like something out of a fairy tale. Although, me having to lay down and get my feet out the water because the horses were pooping and walking, now that was just nasty."

"I have to agree with you on that one, Elyce. It was absolutely awesome and for a change, I was relaxed and so at peace with life. So, let me apologize to everyone for the way I've been acting. I'm sorry," Lana replied.

"It's all good," Tariq said as he gave Lana a bear hug.

"You are squeezing me a little to tight, Tariq."

"That's why it's called a bear hug. It ain't 'spose to feel good." Tariq laughed along with everyone else.

Lana gave him a soft punch in the arm and smiled. It seemed he'd left the drama of their complicated lives back in the city.

"So, Lana, since you're in such a better mood, let's take a walk and chill for a bit." Max grabbed Lana by the hand and pulled her away before she could get her attitude going again.

"Hey, don't y'all disappear too long. We have a boat to catch in three hours. You hear me, Max?" Sienna yelled as they walked away.

"I hear you, Sienna and we'll be on time; or at least, we'll try to be on time. Who knows," he responded.

"For real, Max! The boat leaves in three hours."

"Girl, we'll be there!" Lana interjected holding Max's hand and heading back down towards the beach.

"Babe, I need to eat before we start talking about getting on a boat," Niko told Sienna while rubbing his stomach.

"You always need to eat, Niko. I swear I don't know how you stay so lean." Sienna threw her hands up.

"I works out! By the way fellas, I saw a basketball court when I was out running this morning. We need to get a game in before we leave in a few days."

"You know I'm down man. It's been a minute since we've been on the court." Xavier began doing an air dribble, pull up and jump shot. "And the crowd goes wild!"

"Only in your head man, X."

"Niko, you know I school you chumps every weekend. Don't front."

"We want to play, too," Elyce said.

"No, I don't. What about you, Sienna?"

"Nope. I don't want to play either, Jayce."

“Ugh!” Elyce let out an exasperated sigh and rolled her eyes at her two friends.

“Can you guys, for once, have a sense of adventure or something? We could play the guys for something like,” Elyce pursed her lips together, looked up as if she was thinking really hard about it. “Something like money to hit the spa or go shopping!”

“Ding, ding, ding! I’m in with that plan, girl.”

“Why am I not surprised, Sienna! You in, Jayce?”

“Ball to spa or shop? Why not?” Jayce said in agreement.

The guys stood there looking at them like they had six heads.

“Doc, you don’t really want to play ball against us. It would just be a total massacre. Tariq, Niko, and I would rather not embarrass y’all like that.”

“Wait a minute! Are you saying you don’t think we can play against you all?”

“Yes, Elyce. That’s exactly what I’m saying.”

“Ok, Xavier! Let us get our strategy together and we’ll see you punks on the court tomorrow! Now, let’s go get some food.”

“Thanks for agreeing to this stroll along the beach, Lana. Are you having a good time?”

“I’m having an ok time so far.” Her response to Max was less than enthusiastic.

“Ok, talk to me. What is so terrible that every day we’ve been here, you’ve gotten into with your girls? We’re on vacation. I’m trying to get to know you but you’re making it so difficult.”

Lana let go of Max’s hand, walked over to a beach chair and sat down. He followed her over.

"I don't know, Max. I guess I still feel everyone betrayed me with the whole Tariq and Jayce thing."

"Let me ask you a question. Does it look like your feelings matter to Tariq and Lana?"

"No!"

"Well, you need to recognize that they care deeply for one another and, whether you like it or not, they are going to be a couple. The more you resist, the stronger they'll become. If it's not meant to be, it won't be. But if it is, you need to accept that. Right now, I just want you to accept this."

Max leaned over and kissed Lana. She pulled away and looked at him. He placed his hands on either side of her face and kissed her again. This time, she didn't resist but allowed herself to feel what Max was showing her. That he was indeed trying to get to know her beyond dating.

"How much time do we have before the boat leaves, Max?"

"Two and a half hours now. Why?" Lana raised her right eyebrow, gave Max a sideways look and stood up from her chair.

"Let's go back to the villa; I think it's time I show you how much I appreciate you being here for me and taking the time to get to know me and get inside this stubborn head of mine. You're a good man and I'm feelin' you, Max." He smiled the widest grin ever, took her by the hand and gave it a squeeze.

"My girl!"

26

Elyce snuggled up closer to Xavier running her hands down his broad shoulders, his arms and just over his butt.

"X, you awake?"

"No," he mumbled.

"Wake up then. I want to talk."

"Give me another hour, doc."

"We don't have an hour! I want you to wake up now!" Xavier opened one eye, looked at the clock illuminating 4:30 am. He irritably flipped over to face her.

"What's up, Elyce?"

"I've had an amazing time here with you this week and I just want you to know how much I appreciate all the effort you went through to make this all possible. Not just for me but for everybody who came. My girls being here meant so much to me. I know that you want a relationship with me like we had before. I want that too, but I'm afraid right now. When I love, I love hard and feel like it's only supposed to be just you and me, no side chicks, no other options."

"We've had our differences, doc, and a lot of things have changed in both of our lives. I knew from the first time I saw you in the mall that I could be with you on a serious level. What happened in our past should stay in our past. This trip has been more about me telling you and showing you just how much I am willing to put in the work to be the man that you need." Xavier got nose-to-nose with Elyce and looked her right in her eyes and gave her an Eskimo kiss.

"I've heard you when you've said you'll only be a priority, not an option," Xavier continued, "All I can do is continue to show you that you are just that, today and everyday. Just promise to give me a chance to be all the man you need when we get off this island."

"The island has been exquisite, Xavier. I don't want it to stop."

"But it's the island. We didn't have to do anything we didn't want to do. When we get back, our regular lives are both busy and time consuming. We have to find the time to be about each other and continue to move forward with this relationship that I hope will become so much more. I love you, Elyce Xavier."

Elyce placed her finger over Xavier's lips in a gesture for him not to say anything further. She pushed his right shoulder back towards the bed, so he was lying on his back. Releasing her finger from his mouth, she let her hand travel south hoping to wake the sleeping giant between his legs. She had a quick flash back to her friends on the balcony that night and decided today was the day that she would make love to Xavier like they'd never done before.

Lowering her head and opening her mouth to meet his dick, she gave him slow licks and strokes as he immediately began to harden from her actions. Xavier grabbed a hand full of her hair as her head continued to slowly torture him into ecstasy. He came so quickly, she didn't have time to react so his juices sprayed everywhere, in her mouth, on the bed, in her hair. But she didn't flinch. She continued to stroke him right back up before mounting him backwards, grabbing his ankles and riding him just as she'd rode that stallion days earlier. Xavier was enjoying the view of her nice round ass on top of him rolling back and forth and every so often squeezing her cheeks.

"Shit, babe, tell me again where you learned to do that?"

"I never told you to begin with. Do you like what you see?"

"Oh, hell yes. Don't stop; let me reach over and get my singles."

"Oh no, baby. I'm a grown woman with grown woman bills. I don't take singles, only twenty's or more, sir."

Xavier laughed, lifted her off of him and turned her around to face him.

"You're a real naughty girl, doc. I want to look at you while you ride this dick."

As Elyce began to ride him harder and faster, Xavier was licking and sucking on her nipples and palming her ass so hard at times she thought he was going to leave a mark.

"Faster, baby."

She did as he asked. She could feel her clit rubbing against the top of his shaft. Her body was preparing itself for an explosion.

"Faster! Faster!"

The faster she pumped the more excited he became.

"Shit! Xavier! Shit! Oh damnit. Aaaahhhhh!" Elyce collapsed on top of him but continued to move her hips until he came again.

"Man, if our sex sessions are going to be like this all the time, I may never want to leave the house!"

"Oh, is that what it will take to make you stay, doc? Let me get my ginseng ready when we get back."

They kissed long and hard as she laid on top of him still.

"I believe you really want to show me, Xavier. I believe you."

Before the sun rose, Elyce and Xavier had made love all over the villa from top to bottom. They didn't want to leave paradise any other way.

"I'm so not ready to leave this place. Tariq, let's just stay here and enjoy this island life. I'm sure you can bartend, and I can consult from here. What do you think?" Tariq stood behind Jayce on the balcony holding her from behind as she sipped her morning juice.

"I wouldn't mind staying here but there's a whole world out there that we can explore. Let's do that first, then decide on where we want to settle down. However, before we do any of that, I think you know you need to be my wife, correct?" He turned her around to face him, lifted her chin up so her eyes met his. She smiled, sat her glass down on the patio table and kissed him.

"Yes, I know I'd need to be your wife. I have this sparkler that reminds me of that fact every single day. In fact, as soon as we get back, we should just go to the justice of the peace and do it."

"What? Justice of the peace? What about the big fancy wedding we talked about?"

"I don't need all that, Tariq. I just need you. We can have a reception or party later. My love for you and your love for me is all that matters. Now, we've only got a few hours left before we leave. I need you to come in the shower with me and put it down."

"Is that all you want? You don't ask for much now do you?"

Jayce's robe was hanging off both of her shoulders. Tariq used it to pull her inside the room, especially since they'd already given folks a peep show when they first arrived. He untied her robe at the waist, slipped his hands inside and placed them in the small of her back giving her a gentle rub in a circular motion. She let it drop to the floor as she stood there naked in his arms. He took one hand from her back, traced it along her body until he found her sweet spot and inserted his finger.

"Damn baby, that thang is ready for me."

"She sure is so let's not let this moment pass."

Jayce could feel the bulge in his pants and anxiously untied his pajama pants letting them fall to the floor as well. He picked her up and sat down on the edge of the bed with her legs straddling his.

"Put it in for me, baby," he whispered.

"Gladly."

With one hand around his neck to steady herself, she reached between their legs to grab his dick that was pointing straight out but resting between her ass checks.

He slid inside her with ease due to her wetness.

"Don't move!" she commanded.

"OK."

Jayce dropped her hands to his hips, so she could maneuver herself back and forth watching her creamy residue thicken with every stroke. It felt so good to both of them. She kept going until she came all around his dick.

"Is that all you got, lady?" Tariq asked with a mannish smirk on his face.

"I'm sure you're going to see," Jayce responded.

"Yes, baby, I am going to see what else you have for me. I need you to come at least two more times before we go."

Tariq flipped Jayce over on her back slowly fucking her until her eyes were tightly closed and she was coming again, and he came right along with her.

“That’s two! You owe me one more, J, in the shower like you asked.”

“You know I’m old! I can’t go all day.”

“You might want to tell your pussy that! She says you’re lying!”

27

"I trust everyone has enjoyed their visit with us this week," Remi remarked as she and the other staff filled the room.

"Yes, Remi. Thanks to you and your team, everything was absolutely fabulous. I have a feeling you'll be seeing some or all of us again soon."

"We truly appreciate your business, Mr. Tuft. I'm sorry, I mean Xavier. And we do hope that all of you will join us again."

Elyce walked over and hugged Remi.

"Thank you for being a gracious hostess and giving us all of those options of things to do. This week has really put things in perspective for me."

"I'm glad for you, Elyce. Now, how's me island girl doing? Why me look so sad?" Remi turned to Sienna.

"It's been a really long time since I was last here and visited my family over in St. Maarten. Back then, it wasn't as popular a tourist attraction as it's become. It was about family and love and inexpensive fun. It was just so surreal and a true reminder that my grams is gone to a better place and how the island just leaves you with a strong sense of family. Being able to spend time with my family that still lives here, and my friends getting to know them and know some things about me I'd never share was more than I could ask from. My family treated my friends and my boo like they'd known them all of their lives. I can't wait to go back."

"It was amazing, babe," Niko added. "Thanks for making sure we got over there to see her family, Remi. It made the trip ten times better than what it would have been if she hadn't had a chance to visit with them."

"No problem, Mr. Niko. You guys seem to be missing a few couples, yes?"

"Jayce, Tariq, Lana, and Max hadn't made it down from their rooms yet?" Niko asked.

"Let me have the desk call them up for you guys. I'm sure you don't want to miss your flight back home."

"I don't know, Remi. I think any one of us would be just fine if we were forced to stay here another day, or two or three!" Elyce shared, rubbing Xavier's arm.

"Again, I'm so glad you all had such a pleasurable time. I'll be right back with an update." Remi turned and headed towards the study.

Just as Remi walked away, the late stragglers came waltzing in looking happy as ever.

"Looks like two somebodies got their groove on this morning." Sienna couldn't help but share standing with her legs crossed peering over the top of her sunglasses.

"Sienna, I swear, you're always talking shit!"

"Lana, I swear, you know I'm right. Hell, your ass even has a lot more pep in your damn step. Clearly, you've been getting your back broke 'cause you've been way less bitchy!"

Sienna high fived Max while Lana tried unsuccessfully to break up their contact. Tariq and Jayce were so into each other; they weren't even listening to what was going on around them.

"Your cars are outside to take you to your plane ladies and gentlemen," Remi told the group and the staff grabbed their bags and headed out the open French doors.

Pleasantries were extended all around from everyone thanking Remi again for such a magnificent time and telling her they'd all be back soon. The ride back to the plane was silent as Elyce and Xavier held hands and stared out the window looking at the water along the coast.

"Xavier, promise me we'll take time to go to the beach as often as possible but at least once a year, every year, and I don't mean along the coastline of the USA."

"Sure, Elyce, if you promise me that we'll take a trip really soon to see your parents in St. Croix."

"Uh, that might be a little awkward seeing as I took that asshole there."

"Well, that's in our past. This is our present and our future. Who you were with previously doesn't matter as long as right now, I'm who you are seeing!"

"That part," Elyce added. "Real talk!"

"Good to see you, Captain! I hope you and Cesalie enjoyed your stay here."

"We did have a good time but as you know, we had a few trips in between. How are things with your lady friend, Xavier?"

"Cap, I can't complain. I think we are a lot closer today than when she stepped on this plane a week ago."

"Well, that's good news! No, that's great news! Good luck to you, man." He shook Xavier's hand and patted him on the back.

As the plane was being loaded, the ladies settled themselves onboard while the guys stood outside chatting with Captain Anthony.

"You gorgeous ladies look like you had a good time," Celselie commented as she handed everyone waters for hydration.

"Ceselie, we had a trip that is almost indescribable," Sienna replied. "After this trip, I'm almost sure I'll be married next! Well maybe not next but soon."

"Really now? I guess you ladies gave it to your guys so good they'll want to marry you." Cesalie's hands were on her hips.

The ladies all laughed at her statement.

"Is that what you did to get Captain Anthony? I see how he watches you," Sienna asked.

"Of course it is, Sienna. Women have to be a lady in the streets and a freak in the sheets. It'll get you whatever you want, whenever you want it! Congrats to you all. Can I offer you a glass of wine once we get inflight?"

"Ooooooohhhhh yes," Elyce said. "I'm so tired, I just need a little something to put me to sleep quickly."

"I'll take one, too," Lana added.

The guys and Captain Anthony boarded the jet and closed the door. Cesalie completed all the safety checks.

"Ladies and gentlemen, this is your Captain speaking. We are happy to have you back on board with us this afternoon. Your flight time today is two hours and fifty minutes. Should you need anything during your flight, just press the call button and Cesilie will be happy to assist you. Sit back, relax, and we'll see you in a few hours."

Elyce was asleep before the plane took off from the ground without the glass of wine. She was absolutely exhausted from all the sex she and Xavier had before leaving. She was restless, and her head was moving back and forth.

“What was that noise?”

“What noise are you talking about, Elyce?”

“Xavier, I know I heard something sound like a loud boom. You didn’t hear that?”

“No, I didn’t hear a single thing. You’re hearing things I’m sure.”

“Ladies and Gentlemen, this is Captain Anthony. We’ve had a small engine fire and it looks like we’re going in for a crash landing. Remember your safety instructions and pray for a safe landing.”

“Shit! See there. I told your ass that I heard something!”

“What the fuck is going on?” Max asked.

“We are about to fucking crash, man! This can’t be happening to us. Wake everybody up and get them in position.”

“Hey, hey, wake up! Hurry the fuck up and wake up! We are about to crash, and everyone needs to get in position.” Max was running through the cozy cabin space waking up the other couples. Lana started screaming and praying loudly.

“Lord, if we make it out of this alive, I promise that I will do better by those who love me. I swear.”

“Get down y’all, we are about to hit!” Cesilie yelled.

When Elyce came too, she looked around and everyone was out and bleeding from various parts of their bodies.

“Shit! Shit! Xavier, can you hear me? Xavier?”

She checked for his pulse, but it was very faint. Scrambling to get out of her seat, she checked on Jayce, Tariq, Sienna, Niko, Lana, Max, and Cesilie. Nothing. Everyone was dead except for her and Xavier was barely hanging on.

"What the fuck! This can't be happening. This just can't be how this fairytale week ends. What the fuck!" she screamed again.

"Elyce, Elyce! Wake up. You're having a bad dream."

"What? OMG!" Elyce hugged Xavier tightly. "I don't even want to tell you what that dream was about."

"It must have been really bad, doc."

"It was, Xavier. It really was. Thank goodness it was just a dream and not how this vacation ends. We have so much to look forward to." Xavier looked at her and smiled giving her a gentle forehead kiss.

"Ladies and gentlemen, welcome back to Atlanta. We will be landing shortly, and you can all continue your incredible lives, together."